Wonderwall

Short Stories

route 16

First Published by Route
PO Box 167, Pontefract, WF8 4WW
e-mail: info@route-online.com
web: www.route-online.com

ISBN: 1 901927 24 5

Editors:
Anthony Cropper and Ian Daley

Editorial Support:
Julia Cropper, Isabel Galán, Susana Galán
Roger Green, Tony Maguire, Oliver Mantell, Emily Penn

Cover Design
Andy Campbell
www.absolutelynothing.com

Printed by Bookmarque, Croydon

A catalogue for this book is available from the British Library

Route is an imprint of ID Publishing
www.id-publishing.com

This book was possible thanks to support from
Arts Council England

Inside Wonderwall

Wonderwall: a word without obvious meaning. A psychedelic 1960s film that saw a mad professor drilling holes into the wall of his flat and obsessively peering through into the technicolour exotica of his groovy and swinging neighbours. A 1990s anthem from a gritty northern rock band that caught the mood of a nation with the sing-a-long declaration, 'There are many things that I would like to say to you but I don't know how'. Just how do you define this word, this idea, this wonderwall?

A film. A song. And now, a book – a wondrous collection of stories that cast their gaze to people close at hand; the family member, the friend, the casual acquaintance, the passer-by. People so close we can actually touch them.

Wonderwall is an inquisitive look, a glance, part magical, part inspirational, that sits in the space which connects us to other people. The roads we walk may be winding, the lights that light the way, blinding.

Welcome to Wonderwall.

Contents

Surf Scoter
Crista Ermiya

Vernon was named after the football pools because he was conceived on the day his dad won fifty quid on the no-score draws. It was the last piece of good luck Vernon's dad ever had. Walking home from the pub two weeks after the celebrations were over, he slipped in a puddle and cracked his head on the edge of a jutting-out square of pavement. Blood seeped into the puddle with the rain, creating red ripples that lapped at the feet and paws of a man and a dog out for a late-night walk.

Vernon's mother, Cathy, cursed her dead boyfriend, and pursed her lips tight with contempt and worry. She was forced to open them eight and a half months later, screaming with labour pains. It was Cathy who chose the name Vernon, in memory of the ill-fated pools win; an old-man's name that he was sure to get tormented about at school. Cathy hoped that its connotations of tedium and mediocrity would save him from the reckless path of his late father.

Vernon, on the other hand, always thought of himself as a love child.

'What was my dad like?' he would ask, endlessly, despite the tight-lipped warnings of his mother's face. Mostly, Cathy wouldn't answer. When she did, it was in language Vernon wasn't allowed to use himself.

Once, Cathy nursed a black eye after a fight with a blonde woman who lived three streets away and who had knocked on their door one teatime. Vernon had been eating toast in the kitchen and didn't take any notice of their conversation until he heard the two women screaming curses at each other. He ran into the corridor clutching his toast, dropping crumbs on the lino. Through the open front door Vernon saw his mum and the blonde woman tearing at each other's hair, swearing and punching. A couple of the neighbouring husbands managed to separate them.

One of the nosey next-door wifeys winked at Vernon, who was eight years old.

'And do you take after your dad, with his eye for the birds?'

Vernon didn't know what to say, so just stood there and took a bite out of his toast. 'Aye. I'll bet you do,' said the wifey. 'Men, you're all the bloody same, from eight years old to eighty.'

By this time Cathy had shaken off the men holding her back and was storming back up to the house.

'Get inside, Vernon!' she screamed.

Vernon ran back into the kitchen and pondered the information he had just received about his dad's inclination for birds, while his mum bathed her cuts and held a packet of frozen peas to her eyes. Vernon saw that they were called 'Birds Eye' and from then on declared that peas were his favourite food, even though he disliked the colour green.

At the age of ten, Vernon knew the names of all the sea birds that flocked into Gaunt each summer. At twelve, he could identify all the sea birds along the eastern coast. By the time he was fourteen, he knew all the birds of Britain, including the remote Scottish islands to the north and west. His mum approved.

'He's a quiet lad,' she'd say to the woman who sold the newspapers at the corner shop. 'Only cares about his birds, and listening to his music.'

'Oh, it's the quiet ones you've got to watch out for,' teased the newspaper lady, on auto-pilot.

'Not my Vernon,' Cathy would shake her head. 'Not my boy.'

And she'd pay for her twenty Silk Cut and *Gaunt Gazette* and walk home puffing like an old seagull.

Cathy knew Vernon would never leave her.

***

Now he was seventeen, with an inordinate fondness for waterfowl. His mum had a set of three ornamental ducks nailed to the wall of the sitting room, flying over the television in formation. Vernon had always found this strange, flying but not going anywhere. He started to wish that his mum's flying ducks would disappear, that one morning he would come down for breakfast and find that they had migrated. He wondered what his mum's reaction would be. Not good, he thought. His mum didn't much like the thought of losing anything, whether an umbrella on the bus, a single penny from her purse, or an argument. Everything had to be kept close and under control, including, Vernon knew, himself.

Vernon got a job at the local record store. It wasn't a very good store, but it had existed in Gaunt for years and years on the same site; except now it was a franchise of one of the large chains. It was so small that only two other people worked there apart from Vernon, and that included the manager, Mr Peterson. Cathy hadn't wanted Vernon to get a job at first, but had to concede that they needed the money. Her own job, chambermaid up at the Royal Station Hotel on the seafront, was seasonal, 'like the birds' Vernon had explained to his boss. Mr Peterson nodded. Gaunt people were used to struggling through the winters.

One day, after Vernon had been working in the record store for a couple of months, Mr Peterson said all casual-like, 'I knew your dad, you know.'

Vernon felt himself grow hot and could feel his skin go red.

'Aye,' the man continued. 'Big Ramones fan, your dad.'

This was news indeed.

'The Ramones?' Vernon asked incredulously.

His mum only listened to female crooners with big voices – Whitney Houston, Celine Dion, and recently (Vernon shuddered), Joss Stone. Vernon had to listen to his own music with headphones on so as not to disturb his mum. He usually took a walkman out with him when he was watching the birds on the seafront; often he went out to see the birds just to get away from the *Titanic* soundtrack. His mum was a big fan of *My Heart Will Go On*.

'What about The Clash?' asked Vernon, who loved 70s British punk.

'Oh aye, your dad liked all them bands. But The Ramones were his favourite. Always wanted to go to the States himself. We even thought about going together, you know, mebbes start a band ourselves. San Franciso way, near the coast still, but wi' a chance of sunshine, not like this ball-freezing dump.'

Vernon absorbed this new, unexpected information. He borrowed some Ramones CDs off Mr Peterson. Later in the week he went to the library to use the computers. He googled 'American Punk' and 'San Francisco Birds'. Within a few months he knew the names of all the birds that migrated to the San Francisco Bay estuary. Alongside this, he found out everything he could about the punk scene there, at least, everything that could be gleaned from the internet and from music magazines. Vernon had a gift for focus and details.

Cathy was getting worried.

'You call that rubbish music?' she sneered, when *Rocket to Russia* fell out of his rucksack. But the sneer came out more whiny than she intended, and Vernon winced.

'You never told me Mr Peterson knew my dad,' he challenged her.

Cathy blanched.

'Told you that, did he?' she asked. 'I might've known he'd have not kept his mouth shut.' 'Dad didn't think The Ramones were rubbish,' Vernon said.

'Aye, well, your dad didn't think full stop. But you're not like him son, believe me.'

'Well, mebbes I am, more than you think,' Vernon replied.

His voice was a bit shaky. He wasn't used to answering back to his mum, and she wasn't used to hearing it.

'Where's me tabs?' she asked, pretending not to have heard him.

He found her cigarettes and threw them over to her. He went up to his room, put down his rucksack and got his binoculars out instead.

'Going out to see the birds, pet?' Cathy asked when she saw him downstairs.

Vernon grunted a nod and quickly went out before she could say anything else.

Without telling his mum, Vernon opened a postal saving account with a building society in Newcastle. He used the address of the record store so she wouldn't find out. Within a year, he'd saved enough for a cheap plane ticket to the States and some money to get by for a week or so. After that, he'd have to get work. Vernon also applied for a passport, asking his boss to countersign the unflattering photo-booth pictures. He knew Mr Peterson wouldn't tell anyone.

'Good for you lad,' his boss said, when Vernon told him about wanting a passport. 'It's good for a man to stretch his legs.'

At home, arguments were now flaring up over little things. Vernon was extremely tidy, especially in contrast to Cathy, and was often clearing up her belongings.

'Where's my lipstick?' she'd yell, or 'What happened to that letter

13

from the leccy?' Vernon would point to where he'd carefully placed them. Cathy would flip.

'Just leave my stuff alone can't you? What's wrong with you?'

Vernon didn't care that Cathy was no longer proud of how neat he was, the way she used to be, telling all the neighbours what a good son she had. He knew his mum was starting to get unsettled by his behaviour. Vernon had always been a quiet lad, but these days he could hardly bear to talk to her at all.

On the day his plane tickets arrived from the airline company, Vernon packed up some belongings and folded them into his rucksack. It bulged in odd directions and jutted into his back when he lifted it up. No matter. He could buy a proper suitcase at the airport. Vernon pored over the details of his outward journey. He had to catch a train to London via Newcastle, and then travel on the Underground to connect to Heathrow airport. He decided to catch the very first train out of Gaunt, which would be well before his mum had woken up. Vernon didn't go to sleep that night, just sat on his bed fully clothed, listening to The Ramones through his walkman headphones. An hour or so before dawn he put on his jacket, picked up his rucksack and crept downstairs. His mum's bedroom door was open and he could hear her snoring. Downstairs he paused. It was strange, he had to admit, just leaving like this. He'd never been abroad before, he'd not even been out of Gaunt much, except to Newcastle of course; and once he'd been to Edinburgh on a school trip. Maybe it wasn't such a good idea. His mum would be heartbroken and she wasn't that bad, considering.

As he hesitated in the darkness a glint caught his eye from the sitting room. He walked in and saw the three ornamental flying ducks, outlined in the dark room by the light from the streetlamp. On impulse, Vernon went over to the wall and pulled them off,

14

one by one. They left behind clean un-nicotine-stained duck-shaped patches on the wallpaper. Holding the ducks in the crook of one arm, he let himself out of the house quietly and strolled out into the pre-dawn morning. Instead of walking directly to the train station, he went via the cliff and the sea front. Most people wouldn't be able to see the various birds nesting in the cliff-face but Vernon knew where to look. He stood there on the beach, looking up at the sleeping birds in their nests for about half an hour. He grew cold. Then he shook himself, and walked back up to the road and to the station.

***

There was a knock on Cathy's door.

Cathy opened it to find a postman – not her usual one – standing on the doorstep with a large parcel, wrapped up in brown paper.

'Got a whopper here for you, pet,' he said.

'I can't carry that,' she protested.

'Eh, no worries, it's big but it's light,' he said, handing it over. And it was.

'Ta,' said Cathy and shut the door.

She took the parcel into the living room. It was huge, almost half the size of the coffee table. Cathy squinted at the stamps. Puerto Rico. She shrugged, and started to peel off the brown paper. Underneath was more brown paper, with more stamps - this time from Costa Rica. More peeling off, more brown paper, more stamps: Buenos Aires, Tokyo, Moscow, Prague, Sydney, Manila, Phnom Penh. The parcel unravelled into a smaller and smaller bundle, while the sitting room floor became strewn with more and more torn and crumpled fragments of brown parcel paper, until Cathy was down to what must surely be the last sheet. Beneath her fingers she could feel something hard inside. She could hear and feel edges moving against each other, as if maybe whatever was swaddled inside had broken, or perhaps was made of different parts.

Cathy ripped open the last piece of brown paper. Inside, gleaming up at her, were her three ornamental ducks, well-travelled and gloriously world-weary, to hang back up on the wall.

Significant To Bradley
Michael Nath

Like a pop star, a god, a king or male hooker, Bradley went by one name alone. Was it his first name, or his surname? How come everyone agreed to it? Was it to humour him? Or because we all saw there was something out of the ordinary about Bradley that entitled him to be called the way he wanted – even though he was only a personnel manager in a college in the west of England? Somehow, you felt these were questions you couldn't ask.

There were parts of the town where Bradley would not walk. About a particular area by the old Roman wall, he claimed he had a feeling. I wondered about this. Had he once glimpsed there a scene of ancient violence on a winter night? 'I saw two deserters from the 9th legion, cornered, stripped and shivering; saw them inducted to the traditions of the land.'

About the modernized and airy pedestrian space outside one of the precincts, with its benches and large brick flower beds, Bradley claimed he had another feeling. I saw him walking in a street of shops destroyed by the Luftwaffe fifty-three years ago, where Dorothy Perkins and the House of Cards now traded. This got me thinking delightfully of *Brief Encounter*, women in hats, gents with manners, lipstick, repression, cakes; and cigarettes in those broad cartons.

But Bradley wouldn't give reasons for his feelings about the town. He would just make detours.

Maybe one of us should have said to him, 'Listen up, chum. The sole basis of your superstition is that if you pass the old wall,

19

nothing whatsoever is going to happen. That's why you avoid it. I am telling you this for your own benefit, etc.' But I was enchanted by him; while Davey Henderson was entertained, and tried his best not to scoff. Between us, we made a pretty gentle audience for Bradley's confidences – initially at least.

***

He told us of a dream of serial numbers and theatre tickets, and of a silver teapot that he was not in the habit of using but decided to use the next morning; in which he then found the tickets that he thought he'd lost forever. We listened patiently; and discussed it when he'd gone.

'Did he say he dreamed *of* the teapot?' Henderson asked me.

'Not as such. From what I could make out.' Bradley's narration had seemed longer than I could now remember it. Already details were escaping.

'So what's the point? Tell me.'

'I think what he meant was, the discovery came so soon after the dream, there was something special about it – about the dream.'

'But he must have known he'd lost them anyway – without dreaming about it. You don't realize in a dream you've lost something do you? "Ah, I dreamed last night I lost a fiver. And when I searched my wallet this morning, I had indeed!" Come on!'

'Yeah all right,' I said. 'But it meant something to him.' Henderson could be very destructive at times. I'd known him fifteen years or more; we had no thought of shaking each other off.

'He lost his tickets. He then remembered where he put them. We can do very nicely without the dream.'

Though we'd spent half an hour talking about it.

***

Bradley dressed the part. Another night, he showed us photographs of a recent holiday he'd taken with Trudy (his fiancée) somewhere off the Straits of Messina, in which it was impossible to detect the Brit abroad. In lovely creamy blouses he appeared, long trousers, a basket such as country women carry in hedgerows, and a mysterious Hispanic hat. That was for the day time. In one of the evening pictures, I could have sworn I saw him in a little cloak but he whipped it away.

After he'd gone, Henderson bought me another gin. We always stayed later than Bradley, who had to drive a long way home to Trudy.

***

When we next went out, Bradley told us of a stag weekend (not the exact phrase he used) he'd been on thirteen years ago with a rather close friend of his from college, during which he'd been introduced to a friend of the close friend. In the course of the weekend, Bradley got on very well indeed with the 'under-friend'. So well, in truth, that there'd been no need for any of the sort of promises for the future that people tend to make on such occasions; they hadn't even exchanged phone numbers. Hadn't needed to. It had been a perfect encounter.

And that was that, until last year the rather close friend had died of cancer at the age of only thirty-eight.

At the funeral, Bradley and the under-friend had met again for the first time in thirteen years and the latter had given Bradley a lift to the crematorium. They'd looked at the wreaths together and had a cigarette. Afterwards, they'd each of them gone their own way. Never would they meet again.

'Why not?' Henderson asked. 'Might as well see the boy for a pint, you like him that much.'

'It would be dangerous,' Bradley murmured. I was glad Henderson didn't press the point. Hands trembling slightly, Bradley rolled himself a cigarette, lit it and said, 'There couldn't possibly be an occasion.'

'What are you having?' enquired Henderson, who doubtless wanted to get to the bar so he could laugh.

'I'm afraid I have to go now.'

'Aw come on, Brad!'

'No.' Bradley got up. 'Thanks for listening.'

'That was a bit fucking precious was it not?' Henderson said, Bradley having disappeared.

'Why?'

'Our friendship was too perfect for the world I do declare!' Henderson's Edinburgh accent gave the words a mincing buzz. 'What about the fella who died? No thought for him was there?'

'I don't know.' The story'd made me feel rather left out, in fact painfully so. I took this as a sign of art, and resented Henderson for his shrewdness. 'It was about marriage and death,' I tried to explain. 'That's why they could only meet twice.' My mouth was too dry to repeat Bradley's words, 'There couldn't possibly be another occasion.'

'Why not?'

'Because it wouldn't have been significant.'

'Yerrah! Anything's as significant as you make it.'

'Exactly.'

Henderson threw himself back in his chair as if he'd won the point. But there's more to life than points.

***

It was of terrible significance when Bradley missed the train that crashed in West London towards the end of that summer. He'd been due to go up and attend a seminar the next day, and that was the train he'd had his heart set on, having left his house with just enough time and driven to the station, only to be held up by –

'A traction engine?' Henderson wondered.

'No. Heavy traffic actually,' Bradley said with a faraway look.

I could not point out that Bradley regularly missed trains to London; so often, in fact, that he virtually always travelled by chance. He squinted at me as if we were standing on opposite banks of a river.

'You've cheated death, Brad!' Henderson said, nodding to himself. 'What'll you have?'

'The phone rang just as I was going out the door,' Bradley murmured, ignoring Henderson. 'Usually I'd ignore it if I was in a hurry. I've got my mobile anyway.'

'But this time you answered?'

Bradley nodded.

'Who was it, Brad?'

'I – I can't tell you.'

'That fella you met at the funeral?'

Like a teacher when one of the slower members of the class shows signs of memory but oblivion of the key principles, Bradley shook his head.

'Wrong number?'

'No.' Bradley pouted solemnly.

'Come on, Brad!' Henderson exclaimed. 'Don't hold back on your pals!'

'Another time. Maybe. I'll get these.' He rose.

Henderson grinned. 'He'll tell you. Doesn't trust me.'

'That's because you're a journalist.' I patted Henderson on the arm. 'Think it'll be significant?'

'It'll be as significant as the boy makes it.'

'Exactly.' I could see Bradley at the bar. Tonight he was wearing a green suede top that made me think of Robin Hood, and boots – more of which later. He'd now rejoined us.

'Seven dead plus casualties,' Henderson said. 'You must feel you've got a spirit looking after you!'

Bradley winced like a woman being told how fantastic she looks after she's spent late afternoon and early evening plus part of the morning and the day before making bloody sure she does, narrowed his eyes and said, 'Of course not.'

'Was it just luck then? That what you think, Brad?' I asked patiently.

'All those poor people.' Bradley shook his head. 'I can hardly bear to think about them. Those poor people.'

'Why don't you write to the families?' Henderson asked.

Bradley shook his head: 'That wouldn't be appropriate.' He now made a point of falling out of the conversation, looking round the pub as if expecting certain invited figures to arrive. Then he was finishing his drink, making his excuse to leave.

Henderson winked at me. I went to the bar and bought us another.

Bradley got me alone a couple of weeks later. We both worked at the same place and he'd hung around my desk for much of the late afternoon, complimenting me on this and that, wondering what I was doing this evening, inviting me out for a drink as early as he decently could. He knew now that Henderson, who worked over the other side of town, had no means of getting in touch with me, since I didn't have a mobile. Just to make sure, he took me to a pub by a canal that wasn't likely to be a haunt of mine and Davey, suggesting that we made the most of the fine September weather. He had the boots on again, very sturdy, fawn-coloured, as if made for hard riding: not what you'd expect towards the end of the twentieth century. Cromwell might have worn them. It was as if he expected roads to disappear.

After a few jokes (Bradley was inclined to be humorous when on his own with me, which I loved), he stretched himself in the manner of a bird about to take off from the lawn: 'Why did I miss the train?'

The question irritated me gently. 'Because you were caught in traffic.'

'Before that?' he urged me.

'Because you answered the phone, wasn't it?'

'Who was it on the phone?'

'Well this was what you wouldn't tell us, Brad.'

'Hm.' He nodded, eyes narrowed. 'Same again?'

He was away for some time. A plastic bag and leaves floated by on the canal. The water was like a painted window. I imagined Bradley trampling over it in his boots, finally disappearing into the distance. Then he was behind me with the drinks.

Intense and intimate he sat, rolling a cigarette in preparation. He had a crimson and ochre pouch, different from the sort smoked by anyone else, named after a town in the Lake District. I said nothing. Looking with attention behind me, his face seemed to be losing ownership, as if he'd suddenly moved out in anticipation of an explosive sneeze. Turning my head to follow his gaze, I saw Henderson gliding in our direction in the prow of a small canal cruiser, pretending to examine us through a telescope. Beside him was a Japanese girl in white hotpants with a flower in her hair who was keeping an eye on his footing.

'Now then!' Henderson shouted as they embarked at the pub wharf. 'Fancy seeing you, etc!'

'Same goes for you!'

'Yumi fancied a canal trip,' Henderson said joining us without ceremony and introducing his friend. 'Last one back is not till 11.15,' he grinned.

Bradley spent the rest of the evening in a brave sulk, unable to leave without me and irked by the heartiness of Henderson and his companion, who ordered a pub platter of one dozen sausages of assorted flavours. I joined in the merriment and ate a sausage; but I felt for Bradley. The opportunity of learning the identity of his caller had quite possibly gone forever.

***

He made his final attempt to convince us early one evening in the October of that year. The three of us were drinking in a hotel that had been converted into a vast pub of many bars. Under a glass roof, we sat in a conservatory with large windows that looked down onto sloping gardens and the Great Western Railway. Henderson had been speculating about the barmaid's thong for a good ten minutes when Bradley said, 'I told you about Marc Millner didn't I? Both of you?'

During the summer, he'd mentioned this man, who was engaged in a professional campaign against Trudy so as to block her promotion. Henderson nodded.

'Well he's dead now.' Bradley looked at his fingers, which were trembling. 'Died last weekend.'

'What happened to him?'

'He killed himself.'

'Terrible.'

'Yes,' Bradley said with a suffering ecstatic movement of his eyes. 'I saw him last.'

'How d'you mean?' Henderson demanded.

'Saw him driving north of the moors Friday night.'

'Where were you, Brad?'

'I passed him. In the other direction.'

'Where did he die?'

'At his home. He drove home and died. I saw him last.' We were silent. 'Same again?' Bradley rose and went to the bar. He was wearing a loose black shirt patterned with orange tears and black Chelsea boots as sharp as horns. Henderson muttered something. Henderson probably spent about quarter of an hour a year buying clothes: I never noticed what he was wearing; merely knew he wasn't nude.

'Why d'you dress like a wicked witch?' he asked Bradley, who'd returned with our drinks. Bradley tried to laugh. 'You are a twisted wee nyaff, so you are. You are a sham. If your man Millner killed himself, it had fuck all to do with the fact he spied you on your broomstick as he drove along a country road. Let me advise you of that. Thanks for the drink by the way.'

'I'm afraid you don't understand.' Bradley checked my face then gazed between us.

'Don't understand what?' Henderson was going to see this through, for truth's sake.

'Either you see it or you don't.'

'See *what*?'

Bradley dug his elbows into the table. 'See what I have to tell myself.'

'What about?'

'My significance.'

Henderson grinned with sincere ferocity: 'Let me tell you, my friend, you do not have *any*.'

Bradley's face seemed to leave the pub and become absorbed in a terrible thought. 'Do you mean I've been a joke to you? Both of you?'

I was beginning to say, 'Of course not ...', but Henderson

interrupted: 'That's it, my man. You're an excellent joke!'

'What am I?'

'You've got as much significance as a crinkle-cut chip!' Henderson cackled.

'Come outside!' Bradley was rising.

'What are you going to do? Call up Mephistophilis?'

'Come outside!' Bradley said again. He seemed to be growing. 'Are you frightened?'

'Ah don't be ridiculous!' hawed Henderson, making me a puzzled face.

'Am I a joke or not?' People at adjoining tables were now beholding the spectacle. Bradley took some steps backwards as if he were going to run at Henderson and take a penalty with him; then turned his back and walked out.

Henderson shook his head, simulating confusion. I wished I had the conviction to follow Bradley. Yet I sat there loathing my old friend, as disgusted with myself as the trashiest collaborator.

The White Road
Tania Hershman

What's long, white, and very, very cold? The road to the South Pole is nearing completion... Almost a century after the explorers Amundsen and Scott battled their way from the coast of Antarctica to the South Pole, a US team is heading the same way but constructing a road as they go. Due for completion by March 2005, this road will stretch for more than 1600 kilometres across some of the most inhospitable terrain in the world.

New Scientist,

07 February 2004

Today is one of them really and truly cold days. You're probably thinking cold is cold is cold, either everything's frosty or you're sipping margaritas by the pool in Florida, but let me tell you, there are degrees of freezing. New York got pretty cold in the wintertime, especially for a southern gal. But all the way down here by the Pole, Antarctic minus forty ain't the same as Antarctic minus twenty-five. You need damn hot coffee in both, that's true, you got me there, but there's a different smell to the air, believe me. When I open up for business in the morning of a minus forty, I stand on the doorstep and sniff, with Fluff beside me. I say, Fluff, it's a damn cold one today and she barks, clever damn dog. Then I turn the sign from Closed to Open and set the water boiling for the first lot, who won't be too far down the White Road.

That's what we call it, because that's what it is, all white. Some days, you got to wear them special glasses that they gave out on the

Induction Day before I came down. Two pairs, in case one got broke. They said, Don't look at that snow when it's sunshining or we'll be putting the patch over your eyes, and that'll be enough seeing for you.

Some things the eye shouldn't see. No, some things are just too much for it, if you know what I mean.

Last Wednesday was one of them sunny days they were talking about. It was a real busy morning. I saw the first Ants coming down the road around seven am. That's what I call them, Ants, 'cause that's what they are at first. I'm looking out through my big glass windows, the ones with the special coating on so they never freeze or get misty with all the heat from the guys inside. It's like you're watching a big white TV screen, it's all nothing, nothing, nothing – and then, sudden like, little dots appear: the Ants. They get bigger and bigger, and soon you see them, heading straight for me and my coffee machine. Big red trucks, with all their fancy equipment they carry to the research guys at the Pole a couple of miles past us.

It's probably Phil and Eric, I was thinking, and yeah, they pulled up and stomped in through the snow, stamping their big feet all over the floor, rubbing their hands.

'Whassup, Mags,' shouts one of them, Eric or Phil, never could quite tell the difference.

'Cold, boys?' I ask, same as I always do on a Wednesday when they make their run.

'Freeze ya soon as look at ya,' says the other one, getting stuck trying to pull his snow jacket over his big head.

'Coffee?' I say.

'You're the best, Mags,' they say together, and while they're arranging themselves in a booth, I start the pouring and bring over the cups and a couple of menus.

When I first started, half a year ago, it was quiet; everybody was just wanting to speed down that White Road and get to where it was they were going. But then slowly, they take notice of me and Fluff and our little sign for Last Stop Coffee, and they start slowing down and making my acquaintance. They find us pretty friendly, the coffee's hot and not too bad, and I make the best damn scrambled in about a thousand white miles. I add things to my menu now and again, depending on the supplies I get through once a month when Les brings me a truckload. Sometimes it's fruit he brings me, he got hold of a box of mangos once and you should've heard how everyone was over my mango and sweet potato pie, they just loved it. Sometimes it's nothing more exciting than a whole truckload of tuna and I get to see all the different dishes I can make out of that. I can get pretty inventive with what Les hauls down here. I always was good in the kitchen, my kids'll tell you that, if you can find them. The one who's gone, he loved my scrambled the most. Ate it before it touched the plate, I used to say.

Back to last Wednesday. 'What'll it be?' I'm asking Phil and Eric. They umm and ahh and stare at the menus like they ain't never seen them before, like this ain't the only place for hundreds of miles and they haven't been coming here and eating my food once a week for I don't know how long.

I love doing this, chatting and feeding the hungry. In between one lot and another, Fluff and I'll sit down for a breather, me with my thirty-third coffee of the day most probably, and we'll stare out into the white. You could get lost in all that white. I never knew an outside could look so clean. I thought before I got here that I would miss the colours, the greens and the blues, the yellows and the browns. Not red. I would never miss red.

But I don't miss a thing.

In the evenings we'll watch the TV. We get so many stations on that satellite, my fingers hurt from all that channel-spinning. Fluff'll bark if I do it too much, gives her a headache. She barks and I stop right there on that channel and we watch some soap opera with guys with square chins and names like Ridge, or a bit of the news from the real world, all them disasters and stuff. Then we hit the hay, early to most folks, but we got to get up. I don't mind it, I always was an early bird. Don't want to waste your life, I told my young 'uns, but they didn't listen. Never do. Then, before you know it, it's too late.

Phil, or maybe it's Eric, asks for waffles and maple syrup, and the other one wants toast and jam, and they both drink the coffee like it's coming off the trees tomorrow and that's the end of it.

So I go back into the kitchen and set about it. I stand in front of the toaster and I close my eyes. I reach with my left hand and feel about on the counter top until I find the bread bag, and I grab it and take out two slices with my right. I put the bag down, trying to picture in my head where it is, and I feel over to the toaster. Toast goes in first time! It's because I've been practicing. Every day now for about two months, I've been practicing with my eyes closed, a little every day. Now I can do it. I know where everything is, I can work all my gadgets and stuff.

It was hard at first. I dropped things, I cheated and opened my eyes to clean up eggs and stuff that slid through my fingers. I put the grill on the wrong settings, nearly burned us down, or left things so raw they could walk. But now I got it down, I can do it.

I take Phil and Eric their food, and while they dig in, I sit in the next booth and we chat for a bit.

'We got two tons of gloves today,' they say. 'I don't know what they do down there, all those rubber gloves. Boxes and boxes of them. Some cutting up of stuff, I bet.'

'What else you got,' I ask, sipping my coffee.

'The week's newspapers, like always,' they say. 'Bit old now, but they get so excited when we come in. Doc Baxter, he does all the crosswords. Those guys, they're real smart.'

'They're doing important work,' I say. 'They're checking out the ozone layer and stuff like that, making sure we humans ain't destroying it all too fast. Gotta have someone in these out of the way places, learning about what's going on, increasing the world's know-how, don't you?'

They nod at me, grin, stuff food in their mouths. A few minutes later, they're pulling their layers back on, paying the cheque, and out the door.

The rest of Wednesday morning people are streaming in: different delivery guys, like always, some regulars, some new and in need of serious coffee. And a special lot: a big group of young scientists on their way for a visit. One of them looks so much like... I have to stop myself going over and saying, Hey....

That's when I know it's a sign. It has to be the day.

I knew the afternoon was gonna be quiet. Anyone who comes down here, comes through real early, in case the weather starts with its howling and rough stuff. The sun was out, it's one of them days they told me about. Dazzling, spreading light all over the white.

'It's time,' I say to Fluff. She's real quiet, smart dog. I put on my glasses, snap on her lead, open the door and we step out.

It still amazes me, like it did the first time. I don't think a body would ever get used to it, the soft clean cotton-wool of it all, stretching on and on and on. The road ain't cutting through it, it's part of it, just flattened out a bit. A different white, a little dirty from the cars, but not so that it gets in the way of the beautifulness of it all. I cried the first day I got here. It was like I thought peace would be.

Fluff is stood by me, her head resting next to my knee. I move a few steps towards the sun, making sure I know where the door is that I just came out of.

'It's OK,' I say to her. 'We can do this, you and me. It'll still be me. You know that.' I bend down, take hold of her leash, and straighten up. Then I take off my glasses.

At first I see everything so sharp, and the white looks like gold. My eyes see little bits of gold shining all over the ground, and then it starts moving, like fishes swimming in and out of my head. Then the blurring begins. I feel dizzy, there is this pain behind my eyes, but I keep on staring. I am not going to shut them until it's done, it's over.

I don't know how long I stand there. Slowly, slowly, someone is dropping a cloth over me and this mist comes down in front of my eyes.

Then it's all over. It's all just white.

That was Wednesday and I have to tell you, I'm pretty used to it already. That sure happened quick. I had thought when I first got the idea after watching a programme on the television, three months after I had found Josh and everything, that it would be a big shock to the system. Not seeing sounded so different, like another world. But five days of whiteness and it already feels comfortable, like home. Sure I move around a little slow, with Fluff always there, making sure I know she's with me by giving little barks and rubbing up against me. She's a better person than some humans, that dog; some humans don't deserve to live as much as this dog. She leads me around, pushes me in the right direction, makes sure nothing burns.

At first, everyone was real shocked. I couldn't see their faces but I could hear it clear as day. But, you know, they didn't ask too many questions, and I didn't offer any answers anyway. I think most of them knew my story, about the blood, the bits blown open, the staring dead eyes, the things that I saw, things no-one in this life should see. I think they heard, the way people hear everything, nothing spreading faster than a sad tale, nothing worse than a mother losing a child. Down here, everybody's got a story, everyone's got their reasons for being so far from the world. Mine's just one more to add to the pot.

Les says there's some young girl wants to come help out for a few months. Sounds good to me, she'll be mighty welcome when she gets here. But even with just me doing the serving, they keep on coming, and I keep on scrambling and dishing out the coffee.

I still sit and watch for them, only now I don't see the Ants, I hear them. It's not so different really. It's just very white, and that's the way I like it.

Maggie's Farm
James Bones

Bob Dylan died yesterday, or was it today? It doesn't matter. What matters is he's dead, and he was the last.

He was the last hero I had left, and now he's gone. All my heroes are dead. I'm nineteen years old, and every role model I ever had is deader than prog-rock. John Lennon, Jimi Hendrix, Kurt Cobain, Joe Strummer, and now Dylan. Shit.

I told Joe this on the old railway bridge. 'What about Bowie?' he asked. I never much rated Bowie.

The bridge had been condemned since before we were born, an obsolete structure on an abandoned line. We were standing on the edge of the tracks, leaning on the railings, looking down over the river. Joe was already there when I arrived.

We'd been going to the bridge ever since we were kids. It was where we had smoked our first cigarettes, first got pissed and made our first attempts at rolling joints. When we were in school we were down here almost every night. Now I spend most of the year away at university, Joe works at the chicken factory and we hardly ever go to the bridge.

I hadn't heard from him for months. Then I get a phone call in the middle of the summer holidays; Bob Dylan's dead, let's go to the bridge. And so we began our two-man wake.

After about five cans each the singing started. As Joe tossed an empty into the river he howled the first line of *Knockin' on Heaven's Door*. I yelled the next, and on we went, alternate lines. We sang the choruses together.

When we finished the song the river plunged into eerie quiet, even the sound of the water was dying away. We must have scared off any wildlife within a five-mile radius. Neither of us spoke for a long time. The steely grey sky looked heavy, threatening thunder, a downpour or to fall in on us at any moment. Beyond the tower blocks, in the distance, lightning flashed against the darkening sky. One, two, three, four, five. The sound reached us, rumbling across the bridge like the ghost of a train. On the river's bank the pale trunks and dark leaves of birch trees stood undisturbed.

'Any second now,' I broke the silence, 'it's gonna piss it down.'

Joe snorted and threw another empty can into the river. 'The machine broke down today,' he said, pulling another beer out of the pack, 'it was down for a good hour. The managers were worried we wouldn't deliver on our orders.'

The machine Joe was talking about was the heart of the chicken factory he worked in. Live chickens went in one end. Dead, featherless, blood-drained chickens came out the other.

The first thing I asked Joe when I found out he was working there was, 'Do they run round after they're dead?' Joe snorted out a laugh and told me that the chickens they dealt with were battery farmed and could have problems walking whilst alive, never mind running whilst dead. They could twitch like bastards though.

Joe's job entailed pulling chickens out of the crates they arrived in and shoving their scrawny ankles into little manacles on a conveyor belt. The chickens hang upside down from the belt and pass first through an electrified bath, to stun them, and then on to a device named 'the throat cutter'. Last stop for the chickens is the broiling vat, where they get dipped in scalding water to remove their feathers.

Joe only put the live ones into the machine. The ones that had died on the way, there were always quite a few, went into the 'not-fit-for-human-consumption' bins, to be made into pet food. Nothing is wasted.

I picked up a small stone and threw it into the river. It thunked into the water and I watched the ripples spread across the surface.

'It was weird,' Joe said, 'but when the machine died, I didn't even notice that the squawking had stopped.'

The squawking had really bothered Joe when he first started at the factory. Listening to the death throes of thousands of chickens every day left him a little frayed around the edges. But like an old woman who has lived next to a motorway for years, Joe had become desensitised to the point where he no longer heard it.

Joe told me how, if a chicken was lively enough, it could avoid the electrified bath and even the throat cutter, so that it was alive and clucking when it went into the broiling vat. If I ever get reincarnated, I would not choose to come back as a chicken.

'We all sat round in the staff room for an hour. Then they started handing out the knives.' Joe's expression was blank. He stared vacantly into the distance. The idea of Joe killing a chicken the old fashioned way made me feel a little flakey. All the fun seemed to have been sucked out of the air.

I got the feeling Joe had said all he was going to say. There was no point pushing him, stones don't bleed. I sat in silence, honestly trying to look serious and sympathetic. Joe was quiet for a long time. Taking a swig of his beer he seemed to relax a bit and I could see a smile starting to build up on his face again. Leaning back to look up at the sky he sang, *Born in Red Hook, Brooklyn, in the year of who knows when.*'

I smiled as Joe flung himself into the song. I knew it was his favourite, but always thought it was an odd choice. Dylan had written loads of other songs that were much better. This song always seemed too melancholic and longwinded to me, but *Joey* was Joe's favourite song, possibly of all time, like maybe he actually thought it was about him. He howled the chorus like a wounded animal, as always, he bellowed the line *'Tell 'em it was crazy Joe,'* with obvious relish and the line *'He aint dead, he's just asleep,'* so loud it might have woken Bob up.

He was laughing at himself as he ended the song and leaned back, his elbows on the railings. 'I've gotta get out of that shit-hole,' he said, 'I don't think I can fucking take much more of it.'

I tried to sound reassuring and said, 'Fuck it, something'll come along sooner or later.' Joe just grunted and stared into the distance.

I clapped my hand onto the back of Joe's neck, and his head sank forward a little. *Johnny's in the basement mixin' up the medicine,'* I yelled at him.

'I'm on the pavement thinkin' bout the government,' Joe shouted back.

Lightning forked the sky overhead, thunder cracked and boomed, the rain came down hard and we were singing again.

I pretended not to notice, but Joe's face had been wet before any raindrops hit it.

Love Thy Neighbour

Jennifer Moore

It was that ridiculous book on feng shui that got her started. She'd picked it up in one of the charity shops in Old Town, where some other poor soul had sensibly disposed of it, and spent the next three days devouring it with the single-minded zeal of a religious convert. She became a woman possessed. I'd come back from the shops in the afternoon to find her dragging a bookcase across the floor, hanging those silly wind chime things in doorways or cutting the spiky points off my prized yucca plant. It was all to do with the flow of *chi* or some such nonsense. She couldn't manage the piano on her own though. Apparently our relationship would become stale and loveless if we lived one day longer with it up against the sitting room wall where it had stood for the past six and a half years, so it was imperative that we moved it post-haste into the study. My study.

With the piano gone the wall looked strangely naked. A dark piano-shaped patch marked its absence, a defiant shadow staring out from the sun-bleached expanse of filigree lilac-flowered wallpaper. At one of the darkened seams the paper had begun curling away from the wall. My wife caught hold of it and tugged hard. The whole strip came away in one smooth piece to reveal a crumbling curtain of plaster. She jabbed lightly at it with her fingers and yelped with surprise as her whole fist disappeared into the wall. I got down on my knees next to her and began pulling away at the loose chunks of plaster. There was something strangely deliberate about the hole that emerged. It was circular, the size of a football.

47

'A porthole,' my wife exclaimed excitedly, straining her neck downwards in order to see through it. 'Goodness, you can see right through to next door.'

We had barely spoken to our neighbours in the three months since they moved in. They were new to Eastbourne – some said they'd been living overseas. They were a funny looking couple with their jet black hair and their dark clothes. They tended to keep themselves to themselves and that suited us fine. Still, we couldn't help wondering exactly what they got up to with that strange discordant music that drifted out through their open windows and the high pitched squeals and cries that accompanied it. Sometimes we would catch a sniff of something smoky and exotic coming from their darkened kitchen and pretend that they were cooking up one of our less fortunate neighbours in some dark satanic ritual. We always spoke in whispers as if they might hear.

A porthole into this strange couple's sitting room was too good to miss. I twisted my own head down to ankle level, as my wife moved aside, and peered through. The room, which in its previous owner's time had been an old lady mix of peach dralon and faded chintz, had been painted a deep blood red. Strange carved wooden masks adorned the far wall and in pride of place hung a large ceremonial knife. It must have been three foot in length with a thick curved silver blade. I shivered involuntarily. Perhaps these were not the sort of people to be caught spying on.

Their sitting room door opened and I jerked my head back, cracking it on the bricks and plaster above. Swearing softly to myself I watched as two black denim clad legs approached. I had been spotted. Having decided that staying put was the most dignified approach to what was a rather embarrassing situation, I started planning my speech. *I suppose this must look rather peculiar from where you're standing. We've just been moving the furniture around over on this*

48

side and we found the funniest thing behind the piano. Well you can see for yourself, there's a gaping great hole through our adjoining wall... Perhaps I could regain the moral high ground by offering to cover the expense of having it filled and replastered.

The legs stopped directly in front of my nose. I waited. Nothing happened. The legs turned and retreated back to the other side of the room where they sat their owner down on a black leather sofa. I bent my head further down and a torso and face came into view. Suky Harper was perched on the edge of the sofa leafing through a foreign cookery book.

'What can you see?' my wife hissed.

'Shh,' I mouthed. 'She'll hear you.'

'Oh don't be so wet. Say "hello" then. You don't want her to think we're spying on her.'

'Well we are.'

'Come on, move out the way. I'll do it.'

I wriggled sideways and allowed my wife to take my place. It was a ludicrous sight, that portly paisley-skirted backside thrust up into the air as she manoeuvred herself back down into position.

'Hello? Suky?'

There was no response. What kind of a name was Suky anyway?

'Suky?'

Still nothing.

'SUKY?'

She was almost shouting now. A lesser woman would have given up and moved the piano back but my wife was undeterred.

'Well that's just plain rude,' she snorted, standing back up and dusting herself down. 'I've got a good mind to go round.' And she did.

I took her place at the wall and waited. After a few minutes I saw Suky get up and leave the room. She returned shortly afterwards with my wife in tow. They drew closer, their top halves gradually disappearing from view until just their legs were visible. A familiar sturdy pair of ankles clothed in ten denier flesh-coloured tights stopped just in front of me as the black denim pair had before.

'It's down here,' I heard my wife say. 'Along here somewhere.' A plump middle-aged hand groped its way across the hole.

'That's odd,' she said. 'I could have sworn it was just there.'

The hand was joined by a face. I found myself staring straight into those big blue-grey eyes, blinking myopically at me over the top of her metal-rimmed glasses. Her brow furrowed.

'I don't understand,' she said. 'How very peculiar. I'm...' She faltered, running her eyes from one side to the other as she scanned the wall one last time. I waved furiously.

'I think I'd have noticed a whopping great hole in my wall.' Suky's voice was deep and resentful.

'Yes of course. I'm sorry. I must have been mistaken. I do apologise.'

'Down here,' I shouted as my wife backed slowly out of the room, searching desperately with her eyes. She showed no sign of having heard.

I was still down on my hands and knees when she returned.

'The strangest thing just happened,' she exclaimed as she burst back into our sitting room. 'I told her everything. We looked for the hole and,' she paused for dramatic effect, 'IT WASN'T THERE.'

'I know. I saw you.'

'That whole wall. Completely solid.'

'I know. I heard you. I was waving at you for goodness sake.'

'But that's impossible.'

'Impossible, but true none the less. Look.' I peered through the hole. 'Here comes Angus. Do you think he'd be picking his nose like that if he could see his neighbours staring at him through the wall? It must be one-way only. We could sit and spy on them for hours at a time and they'd never know.'

So we did. It was strangely compulsive, seeing without being seen. It gave us an odd sense of power, of superiority. My wife bought some pale pink scatter cushions which we scattered liberally in front of the hole for propping our chins or elbows on as we lay full length along the floor on our stomachs. Generally we took it in turns. I would make the most of my wife's absence when she went out to her coffee mornings and church committee meetings, spreading myself out fully and enjoying the privacy. Just me, Suky and Angus. I took to working in the afternoons instead, when our neighbours were out. My wife would take the early evening slots when I was finishing off my translations and the evenings were shared between us.

If anything exciting happened, like the time when Suky spilt red wine on the carpet and started wailing and scratching at the skin on her pale thin wrists, then each was duty bound to alert the other at once. Then we would squash up together, side by side in companionable stillness, enjoying the spectacle.

'She wants to put some white wine on that,' my wife had whispered excitedly. Stains made her curiously agitated. 'Perhaps I should go round…'

I pulled her back.

'Leave it. Come on, it's not your problem. Just relax. Enjoy the show.'

It wasn't always exciting of course. There were times when our neighbours simply sat and read or jotted things down on a sleek silver laptop. Sometimes I spent these quiet times dozing, sometimes I would get up and walk around to stretch out my aching limbs but I always returned. We had watched as they moved the armchair round to cover the red wine stain, we had waited patiently for Suky to finish her big round puzzle of the London Eye. We knew instinctively when Angus was irritated, when he was angling for a fight. It would always be something small – the dust on the mantelpiece, the fish bone in his dinner, the curtains left open after dusk. He warmed up with heavy sighs and a knotted brow. Next came the snide remarks, the mild provocation. Suky usually took the bait, rounding on him with a complaint of her own, egging him on. Before long the insults would be flying thick and fast, Angus shouting, Suky wailing. Sometimes anger would get the better of him and he would lash out with his hands. Sometimes Suky would flee the room, sobbing, leaving him sullen and silent on the sofa. Eventually he too would get up and leave. Relations were always restored on their return. I hated those temporary absences, felt keenly their loss. Beyond the limits of their living room they were out of my control and I could only guess at those missing minutes and hours.

We knew so little about their public lives yet the minutiae of their private life belonged wholly to us. We did not know what they did for a living – they certainly didn't keep regular hours – yet we knew about the recurrent mouth ulcer on the inside of Angus's bottom lip, we knew Suky liked to wear her hair in schoolgirl plaits and read Dickens novels stark naked when Angus was out for the evening. I feigned disinterest on those nights, retreating to the kitchen to do the washing up lest my wife take umbrage. There, amidst the pots and pans, I would play the image back at my leisure, revelling in the smoothness of that silver white skin, in every soft sensuous curve.

The best nights though were the dancing nights, as we called them. At the first burst of that strange discordant music we would leave whatever we might have been doing and race to the hole to watch. It was physically uncomfortable with us both squashed up together for so long but the sheer spectacle of their strange mating dance was worth any number of cramps and knotted muscles. On these nights Angus would stand in the middle of the room and begin swaying hypnotically to the music. His eyes were always closed tight and funny little yelps and cries escaped from his lips as the swaying grew faster and more pronounced. Suky always undid her plaits, letting her dark hair hang down over her shoulders. At a predetermined point she would join him in the centre of the room, her hands on his cheeks, swaying with him in perfect time. Her eyes remained open, staring intently into her lover's face, as she too began to moan and cry. They remained like this for anything up to an hour – the same music, the same ritual every time. Then suddenly the music would stop. We would hold our breath as Angus's eyes snapped open and he began to remove his shirt, slowly, deliberately, one careful button at a time. Breathing heavily he stood statue still as Suky scratched her nails deep into his flesh, etching deep red Celtic knots into the white of his skin. Then each of them would bow silently to the masks on the wall before they disappeared out of the room. What went on then, upstairs, we could only guess at but this spectacle alone filled us with a mystic awe, with a quasi-religious wonder that left our skin tingling and our souls burning. At these times we experienced a sense of closeness, of togetherness such as we had never really known in our married life. We were united in our role of witness, lying together in silence on the blue patterned carpet with the pink cushions long after the actors had left the stage.

We might have gone on like this indefinitely. We no longer watched television or listened to the radio. We barely talked about anything outside of the room next door. All thoughts of feng shui were long gone. My wife had started making excuses to the church ladies and missing meetings and I had, for the first time in my life, been turning down work from prospective clients. The movements of our neighbours began to take over ever larger chunks of our own lives. When Suky was ill with a bad cold and spent two whole days in bed we experienced something akin to grief, a strange sense of mourning. We drifted round the house without purpose, counting down the long hours until Angus returned.

Something happened in those two long days, something changed subtly behind the scenes. Suky was sullen and withdrawn when she re-emerged. She spent whole days on the sofa in her black dressing gown, her hair unplaited and tangled, her Dickens left untouched on the coffee table. Angus too was moody and quick to anger. He ate takeaway food in the armchair and played silent games on the silver laptop. They talked in snatched words, without eye contact, never smiling, never touching.

'It's another woman,' my wife concluded. 'You mark my words. It's always another woman.'

Over the next few weeks we watched as things went from bad to worse. Suky started spending whole nights on the sofa too, scarcely moving from one day to the next. Angus was barely there, only returning late at night with yet another takeaway meal to be eaten in furious silence, the leftovers cast aside carelessly. Litter began to collect on the coffee table, stray noodles trailing greasily across the cover of *Bleak House* and little pools of curry sauce solidifying in the gloomy half light of the curtained room. The stereo system gathered dust in the far corner and the strange dances became a distant memory.

What happened next I can neither forgive or forget. We were

called away by another neighbour one night to help in the search for a missing child. The little boy from three doors down had climbed over the wooden fence at the back of the garden while his mother had been collecting washing in off the line. She had turned her back for just a moment, she said, and when she looked again he had gone. Of course they panicked, running up and down the street and the little alleyway along the back of the Edwardian terrace, screaming his name and calling on everybody they knew to join in the search.

'Just leave it,' I'd begged my wife as the doorbell rang for the third time. 'Pretend we're out.' It was my turn to watch and I didn't want any interruptions.

'We can't,' she'd sighed getting to her feet. 'The car's parked outside and the lights are all on. They can see we're here.'

She went to answer the door. I heard a babble of excited voices and when she came back in she was carrying our coats.

'I'm sorry,' she said. 'Hilary's little boy has run off. They're frantic. I said we'd go and help them look.'

One and a half hours later the boy was discovered curled up fast asleep behind a bush in the corner of his own garden. He had been hiding, he told the now sizable crowd who had gathered at the back of his house, and had dropped off. At the sight of his weeping parents he too started crying and everyone else went home. The poor excuse for a crisis was over.

I paused outside our house, listening. I thought I could hear the strange music from next door. I rushed inside and headed straight to the hole, without even stopping to take off my coat. The music was loud now, louder than usual. My wife followed close behind.

'They must have made up,' she cried breathlessly, kicking off her shoes as she ran.

We flung ourselves onto the cushions and peered in. Angus was lying on the floor in the middle of the room, shirtless. Blood was still pumping out of the heavy red gashes on his chest. Suky was sprawled on the sofa, thick ribbons of red emblazoned crudely across her wrists. Along the back of the sofa lay the big silver knife, blade side up. The carved wooden masks looked down from the wall in silent approval.

We lay there motionless for what felt like forever. It was too much to take in. How could this have happened? How could they have done this? How could we have missed it? I felt something like hatred bubbling up in my chest at the memory of that little boy curled up in the bush. Thanks to his stupidity, thanks to the blind selfishness of his whining parents, we had missed what was quite possibly the greatest event in our neighbours' lives. All that was left to us now was to sit and wait for the ambulance, for the police. They would take them away, my poor pale-skinned Suky and angry overbearing Angus. They would turn the house upside down looking for answers. They would find the porthole. We would have to go back to living our own lives instead.

Rainbows Seen From The Air Are Complete Circles

Sarah Butler

He noticed her coat first – bright cinnabar red, with a slight sheen, and a button hanging on by a single thread; then her hair – greasy stripes of black, turquoise and lilac; and then her legs – stretching out from beneath the coat: bare, pallid, a little too thin.

'Bacon'll be three minutes.' The owner of the café – with its white tiled floor, regimented rows of fixed tables, red plastic chairs, smell of oil - stood where he always did, at the till, a chewed up plastic pen between his teeth, a bright white apron tied around his stomach. 'I'll bring it over.'

'I'll wait.' The customer, who had noticed a red coat before bare legs, stepped aside and gestured with one hand – yellowed fingernails like old parchment – for the girl to go in front. She eased past and scanned the menu board's stumpy black letters. She was suddenly hungry.

'Full English,' she said, tucking her hair behind her ears; pretending not to notice that the customer who'd let her past was staring at her. You draw attention to yourself. Wear some normal fucking clothes. Another man's voice grated against her memory.

'Scrambled or fried?'

'Scrambled. And tea.'

'Four pounds, Miss.'

The customer watched her fumble in a small black handbag; noticed a line of make-up around the edge of her jawline, a pulse hammering at her neck. She pulled out a creased five pound note and handed it over. He stepped closer, closed his fingers around the

59

button and gave a sharp tug. She turned and stepped away, but the button was already safely in the crease of his palm.

'Actually, I'll get a seat,' he said to the owner, turning away from the girl. Someone was in his place. He curled the hand holding the button into a tighter fist and took the table next to his usual one; glared at the old couple who had usurped him. They exchanged glances and continued eating – greasy orange beans, straw coloured hash browns. He slotted himself into place, the blue plastic table just inches above his thighs. The button imprinted its shape into his palm.

He didn't see her approach. He didn't hear the click of patent orange shoes across the tiled floor, or her nervous intakes of breath through narrow nostrils, both studded with silver circles. The first thing he noticed was the clatter of cutlery on the table top – his table top, and a flash of red coat.

'I'm sorry, this is…' He looked up and saw her – eyelids layered with bottle-green make-up, lips outlined scarlet, hand outstretched. 'It's taken,' he spluttered.

She stood, tall on her heels, the pulse still visible at her neck, said nothing.

'I don't usually…' He stared at her palm, white as her legs, like an oyster forced open.

She sat down and put her hand palm down on the table, revealing five different coloured nails – crimson, crocus yellow, emerald, magenta, cobalt blue - the varnish chipped and shrunk.

'I like your nails.' He slammed his lips shut.

'Why did you take it?'

The button burned in his palm. He slipped it into his pocket. 'Take what?'

'You pulled the button off.' She yanked up her coat, shook it at him – a snapped red thread. 'What kind of a weirdo does that?'

'I don't know what you…'

'Empty your pockets.'

She sounded so like a school teacher he found himself obeying her. He pulled a ragged tissue, a two pence coin, a bus ticket and a red button from his pocket and placed them on the table. She picked up the button between her finger – crocus yellow – and thumb – crimson.

'What d'you want a button for?'

'It was about to fall off.'

'Why did you want it?'

He didn't look clean, she decided, staring at him. Thin semi-circles of dirt nestled beneath each fingernail and his skin had a grey, exhausted look. In the other way too, no doubt.

'I'm having a bad enough day,' she said, 'without nutters trying to steal my stuff.'

'I'm sorry.'

She looked at the button for a moment, tucked it into her coat pocket.

'Two full English, one with extra bacon, two teas.' A bored looking waitress, thick dark lips pursed into a sullen pout, unloaded her tray.

'We're not…' he started to say, but the waitress walked away. She had a full, but firm, arse that pulled up the back of her skirt, revealed thick thighs the colour of strong tea. The girl watched her. I like my girls thin – the other man's voice again, like stinging nettles in her mind. On good days he lifted her into his arms and spun her round, feet off the ground, like flying. On bad days she felt brittle, ready to snap. She looked at the man opposite her. He wore a pale grey jumper, the colour of pigeon feathers, which curved over a large stomach. The most striking thing about his face was his cheeks, she decided: wide expanses of flesh like old car leathers, his small features almost lost amongst them. She tore open two paper packets of sugar and tipped them into her tea; watched him spear a wrinkled looking mushroom, and dip it into his beans.

'I liked the colour,' he said; slipped the mushroom into his mouth.

She stirred her tea slowly.

'It's cinnabar,' he said.

'You what?'

'I'd call that colour cinnabar. It's a mineral.' He lowered his head, cut a piece of curled bacon in half. 'And a moth.' He kept his head down, heard her slow intake of breath. Stupid thing to say, fat old man trying to chat up a young girl – get arrested for less; lynched; laughed at.

'It's a nice name,' she said. He looked up. A tear hesitated at the edge of her eye before toppling over to trace a thin wet line down a foundation-caked cheek.

'Are you okay?'

She sniffed and brushed a hand against her face as though wiping something away. 'I'm fine.' She shovelled a large forkful of food into her mouth and chewed noisily. 'You like colours then?' she said, displaying a soft yellow mush on her tongue.

'I collect them.' Again he pressed his lips closed, but too late. Words escaping.

'Right.' She nodded, forked more food into her mouth. 'Right.'

He lifted his fingers to his nose – that smell, always that smell. Heat escaped from his breakfast in thin swirls of steam. He didn't feel hungry. He watched her eat – a swift cleansing of her plate.

'Don't you want that?'

He pushed it towards her. 'You're thin,' he said, 'to eat that much.'

She shrugged, bony shoulders under the red sheen of her coat.

'I'm hungry.'

'What do you do?'

She paused, frozen like those people-statues in Covent Garden, who want money before they'll move. 'I'm a singer.' She tossed her head back, streaks of colour around her painted face. 'With an agent and all…'cept…' She dragged her fork through the remains of his baked beans. 'He says I'm good.' She nodded. 'I can make it.'

'What do you sing?'

That shrug again. 'Whatever, jazz, pop stuff.' She hesitated, looked at him. Grey skin, but his eyes were the same pale pale blue as the cat she'd had, once. 'When I was a kid…' She stopped, but he was looking at her like he wanted to know. 'I used to love church music. You know, choirs and stuff.'

He nodded.

'My mum thought I was mad, going off to church every Sunday, but it was for that music, like angels up in the ceiling.' Another tear threatened to fall. She willed it away. 'My make-up all right?'

He blinked like a frightened animal. 'Fine. It's fine.'

She stared into the bottom of her cup, at its pale brown deposit of sugar granules.

'Can I see?' she asked.

'What?'

'Your collection.'

She followed him down Kentish Town Road, past clogged up lines of traffic, past the Russian man, who sold vegetables outside the tube station, arranging his boxes of potatoes, mushrooms, red peppers like plastic toys.

'It's just down here, not far.' He walked quickly, spoke with a shyness that also contained excitement, an expectation. Like all the rest of them: desperate to touch. She could walk away, but something held her, a laziness, a curiosity, a reluctance to go back to the flat and be faced with questions: Where? Why? With who?

A first floor flat – four grimy steps up to a black front door, paint peeling like bad skin. The entrance smelt like an old people's home – musty and damp. A thin grey carpet gaped away from the walls, revealed gashes of wood at the edges of the stairs. She followed him into a tiny hallway – turquoise carpet, bare walls.

'Don't you heat this place?' She pulled her coat tighter.

He shrugged. 'I don't feel it much.' A hand snaking towards his stomach. 'Do you want tea?'

'Yes.'

'Go in.' He waved her towards an open door. 'Have a look.'

It was a reasonable sized room. A studio – with a single bed skulking by the window, a sofa and a small desk, a wooden chair with one of the slats missing. The pale carpet had three crease lines scored across it, and was scattered with stains. It was the walls that took her breath away. She walked into the middle of the room and turned round and round until the colours started to swirl into each other. It reminded her of the time her grandmother had taken her into Hamley's, told her she could pick anything she wanted as a birthday present. There was that same heady rush of wonder and possibility.

She had never seen so much colour in one space. It was densest at chest height, about a half-metre tall stretch of colour circling the entire room. It stretched up and down in varying degrees, creating an undulating sweep across pasty white walls. Feathers, torn pieces of paper, snatches of material, a leaf, the label from a tin of baked beans, a pen top, silver foil, a video membership card, wrapping paper, pictures of flowers, cars and women cut from glossy magazines, an acorn, pieces of chalk, a toothbrush, a tiny pink

Mexican worry doll, buttons. She ran her fingers across them, not quite touching, cataloguing. She had read once that rainbows, seen from the air, are complete circles. This, then, must be like standing inside that circle, except the colours were made from bits of tat, things stolen from everyday life and turned into something else.

'Two sugars, that's right?' He stood beside her, holding out a cup of tea in a dark blue mug.

She took it, cupped her hands around its warmth and continued to stare at the walls.

'What do you think?' That shy excitement again.

'It's weird. It's like that film…about the guy that collects the photos.'

'I don't watch films much.' He sounded disappointed.

'It's about a guy who works in a photo booth and keeps copies of this family's photos. You're like that…'cept you take stuff from more people.'

'I'm sorry about the button. I don't usually…'

'You'll land up in trouble, ripping ladies' clothing in public.'

He felt the blush spread up from his neck. She must be laughing at him. He imagined her telling the boyfriend, the agent, their heads bent together, then arching back in mirth. Sad old man collects bits of rubbish. Weird.

'It's nice tea.' She smiled at him over her mug. He felt the blush deepen. Brick-red. Pillar-box red. Cherry.

'Sit, please.' He gestured to the sofa, moved quickly to pick up his overalls, dump them on the bed.

She sat, pale legs crossed like twined tree branches. 'You a builder?'

He shook his head, mumbled into his collar.

'What?'

'I collect bins.' He studied his hands, skin yellowed and callused. 'Can you smell it?'

She shuffled across the sofa, put her nose against the curve of his neck and breathed in deeply. 'No.'

She smelt of cheap soap and peppermint chewing-gum. Her breath was warm against his skin.

'I smell it all the time, even once I've showered.'

'Do you take things from the bins?' She moved away and it was as though there was suddenly less air in the room. Her eyes flickered across the walls.

'Not from the bins, no.'

'Where then?'

He shrugged. 'I walk around. I pick things up.'

'Or steal them.' She smiled and he felt the edges of his mouth tug upwards in response.

'Sometimes.'

He wanted to tell her. Everything had its own story. The blonde woman chewing her nails in the doctor's waiting room who left behind a single strand of hair; the boy on Hampstead Heath who'd solemnly handed him an acorn and told him it would grow into a tree if he planted it in his garden – except he didn't have a garden; the woman who'd dropped her video card and shied away, her hand held up as if warding off evil, when he tried to stop her and give it back.

He wanted to touch her. Lifted up his hand to do just that, but stopped when she turned.

'You wear a lot of make-up,' he said, returning his hand to his lap.

'Nothing wrong with that.'

'Would you take it off?'

He saw the panic flash across her eyes. 'You are weird, man. I'd better go.' She made to stand up, unfurling her legs, tugging at her skirt hem.

'I don't want…I just wanted to see.'

She stood, marched across the room and out of the door. He stayed where he was, tipped his head back and closed his eyes.

She stopped with her hand on the front door latch, imagined herself opening it, slamming it shut, walking down the road with her heels clattering against the concrete. Back to him. She held her breath, waiting. Nothing. The man in the room with his crazy collection of colours did nothing. She let herself open the door to the kitchen, walk towards the sink and turn on the cold tap. She scooped water into her palms and rubbed it against her face. Her make-up resisted. Her tears mixed up with the icy water, and chemicals slicked between her fingers. It made her eyes sting. It made her choke. She kept on rubbing; eventually lifted up her face and groped blindly for a towel. She found kitchen roll and pulled off four squares, which she pressed against her skin, felt it soak up water and discarded colour, turn to a soggy mess in her palm. When she walked back into the room he was sitting where she had left him, his eyes closed, his hands resting on his stomach.

He opened his eyes and saw her, red coat, orange shoes, make-up streaked in lines of black, red and green across her face. A bruise flowered across the top of her right cheek bone. He stood quickly, wiped sweating palms against his trousers. He lifted a hand towards her face and she flinched away.

'I won't…I'm sorry.' And then, 'It's amethyst. Amethyst and sapphire.' He brushed his fingertips across the bruise, heard her noisy intake of breath. 'And here, just a hint of topaz.'

'There are more,' she said.

'Show me.'

It was like a shutter slamming. Her eyes turned cold and she held a hand up to cover her cheek. 'You see. You're the same as all of them. Just want to get in my pants.'

He shook his head.

She unbuttoned her coat, watching his eyes all the time. Lust, yes, but something else too. He – the other man – would assume it anyway. Nothing to lose. She shed her clothes, like multi-coloured petals. Stood and waited.

She was like a child - scrawny limbs, pale skin, her breasts faint swells of flesh. The bruises were carefully placed, where it wouldn't show. A history of mustard yellow through to deep plum. He felt tears prick at his eyes, his penis stir in his trousers. So long since he had touched.

'How old are you?' he asked.

She shrugged. 'Old enough.'

'Will you lie down?'

She lay on the floor, her eyes squeezed shut as though in pain. He knelt beside her and waited. The traffic noise outside was constant: a heaving, growling stream of cars he barely noticed anymore. He listened to it now, heard too the muffled song of a bird.

'What's your favourite bird?' he asked.

She opened her eyes. 'I told you, you're weird,' she said, half sitting and raising a hand to cover her breasts.

'Don't you have one?'

She rolled her eyes upwards. 'I don't know, a parrot. Yes, a parrot, but not one in a cage.' She paused; looked at him. 'You know, I've seen some on Hampstead Heath. Green ones. I swear. Green feathers up in a tree. You should go, collect some.'

He nodded, said nothing.

'So what's yours?'

'A sparrow. Can I touch you?'

'You're a colour freak and you like sparrows?'

'Have you ever looked at one?'

'Yeah.'

'Really?'

'For fuck's sake, can we get on with this?' She lay back and stared at the ceiling, shifted her legs slightly apart. She'd give this weirdo a bit of comfort, something to tell his mates about, not that they'd believe him. She could feel goose pimples crawl across her skin, turn her nipples hard. He knelt by her, breathing heavily. Poor fucker, probably hadn't got it on in years. She closed her eyes and waited.

He started with the one on her face, ran his fingertip in curling circles out from the middle. She felt him move down her body and each time he stopped, she almost told him: that's when I fell asleep instead of making dinner; that's when I said I was too tired; that's when I got a cold and couldn't sing in his stupid concert; that's when I was late home; that's when he thought I was fucking his friend; that was just for the hell of it. Stories etched onto her skin, and behind them, round them, memories of other stories. When he reached the last one, he went back to the first. It made her sleepy.

'What do you want?' he said.

She opened her eyes, blinking into the light. 'Whatever.'

He saw it again, shutters slammed across her eyes. 'Do you want to sleep?'

A faint nod. He picked her up and carried her to the bed, pushed the overalls onto the floor. Light as a feather. She fell asleep, her thumb lodged between her teeth. He sat, and watched her, stroked her hair and the ugly bruise on her cheek.

She woke in a strange bed, inside a circle of colour. Grey morning light seeped through thin yellow curtains. She was naked under a scratchy grey blanket. Her clothes had been neatly folded and placed on the wooden chair. He wasn't there. She lay and remembered his fingers tracing whorls over her bruises. Get up. Get the fuck out of here. He is going to go ballistic. She lay a while longer, staring at this man's collection of other people's rubbish, mislaid pieces of lives. She tried to remember what he looked like, but could only picture a pigeon-grey jumper and wide, lined cheeks. The overalls were gone. He must be at work, collecting neatly knotted plastic bags bulging with waste. She made herself roll out of bed. On top of her clothes lay an envelope – used, the seal unevenly torn - on the back of which was written 'You can stay'. She moved it aside and dressed quickly, hands shaking as she layered the colours over her skin. Time for another day. Explanation, fight, make up. She pushed both hands into her jacket pockets, and felt the smooth surface of a red button. On the desk sat a small tube of glue. She squeezed it onto the back of the button, and pressed it into place amongst the reds – between a creased piece of ribbon and a curl of wool; closed the door behind her.

Mr Sam The Spaceman
Philip Hancock

Day 1

Sam snapped back the ignition key, killing the radio before the eight o'clock news bulletin. Stepping from the warmth of his minivan he faced the playground equipment at Radnor Walk. The seats of the swings were out of reach, their chains coiled around the high crossbar. The paved area beneath them and surrounding the slide, roundabout and climbing frame was littered with roach ends. A bloodied syringe jutted from one of the steps to the slide and amongst the glitter of jagged glass, Stella Artois tins rattled in the breeze.

The facelift of the equipment was specified to take three working days. The slide was to be repainted in four bright colours: red for its steps; yellow on the handrails; blue for its turret and stanchions; and green on the slide's casing. Sam's clean scraper sliced through the scabs of rust, dew seeped over its blade as he flicked them clear. At ten-thirty, he stepped back and smiled. The red oxide spot-primer had given the slide the appearance of measles. He was getting on well and felt confident that he'd be finished on the third day before lunchtime.

Checking over the climbing frame, Sam paused at the sudden rise and fall of voices. A boy dressed in denim dungarees darted across his view. A young woman wearing an ecru cloche hat and a checked duffel coat lagged behind him. Her face was pale and she was as thin as grated cheese. The boy turned to her and pointed up at the swings. Shaking her head, she reached for his hand. As the boy hugged her legs, she lifted her face.

'Excuse me,' she called, stepping towards the climbing frame. 'He wants to go on the swings.' The boy had taken to kicking at a tuft of rough grass. 'Could you help me, please?'

'Just a sec, duck,' Sam replied, stooping beneath the cold bars to face her.

The Kangol cloche hat she was wearing partly shaded her still eyes and high cheekbones. Her hair was drawn snugly to the front of her neck in two dusky red pigtails.

'I may as well drop all of 'em while I'm at it,' Sam sighed, opening out his stepladder. He winked at the boy who snuggled into the woman's unfastened coat. 'Hello, little man.'

'He's gone shy,' she said, fingering his shiny hair. 'Haven't you?'

Sam struggled to free the mangled swings. 'Mind him, duck,' he warned. The chains rattled and a blue seat spiralled downwards. When the fourth swing had steadied, Sam nodded at the boy. 'There you go, sunshine. Three for you, and one for the lovely lady.'

She half-looked to Sam, then down at the boy. 'Say thank you to the mister.'

The boy murmured from her shelter.

Returning from his van with a kettle of grey undercoat, Sam began painting the angular stanchions underneath the slide. He glanced at the young woman as she rocked on the pink swing. She appeared to be in a daze. Her head was bowed and she was focused on her feet. She flicked nervously at a cigarette whilst her left hand was shoved deep inside her patched pocket. The boy had gathered momentum on the blue swing, his tummy pressing upon its hard seat.

The undercoating of the slide came together quickly. Moving on to the rocket-shaped climbing frame, its maze of bars proved tricky to manoeuvre between. It seemed only minutes that Sam had been scraping them free of flaking paint when he jolted to the woman's voice.

'Sorry. Sorry to be a pain,' she pleaded. 'But have you seen the state of the roundabout?'

I'll never get on at this rate, he thought.

Cellulose vapour lingered from the anarchy signs recently sprayed upon the roundabout's wooden panelling, the discarded canister popping up from the bitter grass. Sharp grit and clods of earth lay scattered upon its segmented turntable.

'Bloody vandals!' Sam cursed. 'What a world we live in, eh?'

The woman drew the boy to one side. 'Just look. You're filthy now,' she fussed, patting his trousers.

After wiping the roundabout clean, Sam lifted the boy and perched him on the seat. 'Come on then, sonny Jim,' he enthused. 'D'you want me to give you a little shove?'

The boy tensed his fingers round the handrails.

'Hold tightly.'

Kicking his legs, he squealed as the roundabout picked up speed.

'BOO!' Sam barked, each time he whizzed by.

'Mummy look!'

Sam glimpsed the woman's profile. She couldn't have been much older than her late teens.

'BOO!'

She forced a smile. Delving inside the slip breast pocket of her duffel coat, she pulled out a crushed cigarette packet. 'Want one?'

'No ta, duck. I've never smoked.'

'They're menthol.'

'Mental?' Sam quipped.

'Please yourself,' she replied, curtly.

Sam nodded to the climbing frame. 'I'd better crack on.'

She offered no expression.

'I'm getting the rocket ready,' he tittered.

Only then did they hold each other's eyes. A second attempt to smile almost cracked her sullenness: the way she held herself, her flat responses. Sam was enchanted by the contrast. Maybe she was suspicious of him, or maybe she just thought him stupid. She could be like that Kate Moss, he thought. Better.

'Come on then, you,' she ordered.

The boy sprang from the footplate of the roundabout and ran ahead. 'Bye-bye,' he called, waving to Sam.

Sam watched them disappear from view, along the red rutted track that led to the busy main road.

Day 2

'BOO!'

'What the…!' Sam gasped, turning sharply around.

'Hiya.'

'Oh, it's…' he stammered. 'He…He made me jump.'

'He's been creating mither all morning,' the young woman moaned, pacing behind him.

Sam paused and allowed his eyes to follow her. She looked so different. She was dressed completely in black: a figure-hugging blouse and needle corduroys, contrasting her complexion. Her dyed red hair was combed in a fringe. 'Just watch as he doesn't get any paint on him, duck. The roundabout and these handrails on the slide here are still wet.'

Seeing her spruced up, Sam felt worthless dressed in his filthy overalls. The patter of the boy's feet quickly diverted his attention.

'Mister?' the boy asked, hesitantly. 'Mummy says, please can I go on the slide?'

'Only if you tell me your name first.'

'Ben.'

'And how old is Ben?'

'I'm four.'

'Four?' Sam beamed. 'Wow! I used to be four.'

Ben's face formed a picture of concentration upon the sea-green gloss paint flowing from Sam's brush.

'Is that your mummy?'

He nodded. 'What's your name?'

'Sam.'

'Who are you?'

Sam smiled before delivering the answer he always gave to young children when working on schools. 'I'm a spaceman.'

'Are you?'

'Yep. That's my space rocket,' he said, gesturing towards the climbing frame.

Ben remained transfixed on the shiny paint. 'What are you doing?'

'I'm having a bath.'

Ben giggled. 'You're not having a bath.'

'I am.'

It was at that point, that the woman interjected. 'Is he holding you up, mate?'

'You're not a spaceman,' Ben cried, running for the steps to the slide.

'Ah, he's all right, duck.'

'You're silly. Silly Billy!'

'Ben! Don't you be so rude!'

'Sorry, I forgot,' Sam called to the woman. 'I'm Sam. I'm not a spaceman really, although that climbing frame could well be my Starship Enterprise!'

She raised her eyebrows.

'I mean, it's snazzier than my poor old minivan, don't you think?'

The bridge of her fine nose crinkled and she started to laugh. 'I'm Sarah.'

Ben tottered towards them holding out his hands. They were covered in paint. 'Mister Sam?'

Her laughter stopped as quickly as it began. 'What have I just told you? I'll bloody crown you!'

Sam looked hard at her. Letting out a huff, she strode off towards the swings. Sam crouched in front of Ben. 'Mr Sam's got some magic potion that cleans paint off,' he said, softly. 'I'll take you on the slide in a bit. Would you like that?'

Ben nodded.

'It'll be all right. Show me your handy.'

'I don't like Mummy when she shouts.' Ben sobbed. 'When she cries I want to kiss her and make her better.' Tears hung from his chin like dewdrops. 'There's a black and white cat at the end of my street and when it sees me it runs to me and I stroke it and it's soft and nice like Mummy.'

Sarah appeared much calmer when she returned with a tissue from her bag. 'Will he be all right?'

'He'll be fine. Won't you, buster? It's only a bit of paint.'

Sarah watched as Sam gently wiped Ben's fingers. When they were clean again, Ben turned and hugged her.

'Hang on a tick,' said Sam. 'I've got something for him in the van.'

They watched Ben – silent for the first time – his mouth full of chocolate. 'Thanks,' said Sarah, folding her arms. 'I'm sorry for snapping like that. He should be at the nursery really. I went to fetch him last week and he was dead upset. They knocked his little house down with their tricycles. He's got a couple of bruises on his legs and some buttons were missing from the shoulder of his jumper as well. I'm a bit worried to be honest with you.'

Her words cut into Sam. 'Who?'

'Oh, the kids, y'know. Mind you, the neighbours are just as bad. Always stickin' their soddin' noses in.'

'I'm sorry,' Sam offered, looking to the ground.

'Come on then, little man. Are you ready?'

Sarah's eyes widened. 'Ready for what?'

She watched as Sam ushered Ben to the top of the slide. Carefully, he lifted Ben and rested him on his lap. 'Ready?'

Ben looked nervous.

Holding him close, Sam could smell the freshness of Ben's thick hair. The scent of his soft woollen sweater reminded him of the days when his mother did his washing. 'One. Two. Three.' The world whooshed past them as they whizzed down the slide, to where Sarah was waiting with open arms.

'Another go!' Ben cried. 'Another go!'

Again Sam helped Ben climb the steps to the slide, making sure he kept clear of the newly painted sections. Sarah's face was one of a perfect holiday snapshot.

'Take Mummy on the slide,' Ben shouted. 'Take Mummy on the slide, Mr Sam.'

Sam looked to Sarah, and rolled his eyes.

'Mummy's going to come on my space ship instead,' he laughed. 'I'll be finished paintin' it tomorrow. Then we'll be off.'

Sarah offered a half smile.

'What's it like in space, Mr Sam?'

'Well, it's like this big place where everyone's happy and nice to each other. There's no mither in space. There are lots of toys to play with and nobody tries to break them. You can touch the stars as well. The cats and dogs talk to each other and the birds come down to visit me when I'm having my breakfast.'

Ben's eyes didn't blink.

'There's perfect skies and magic pies,' Sam warbled. 'I'll be off there in my space rocket tomorrow.'

'What are you like?' Sarah said, catching Sam's eye.

'Well, that's not goin' to get us far, is it?' he quipped, nodding to the rickety minivan.

Her expression changed. Her face contracted, as though a cloud had drawn across the sun.

'Sorry, duck. I didn't mean it like that. I was jus'…'

'It's okay,' she said, without emotion, before facing away.

'Might as well be in space. It's gotta be better than livin' round 'ere,' he tried, aware of the awkward pause. 'All I'm ever doin's tryin' to make things good again.'

'We'd better be going,' Sarah said firmly.

'You be a good man for your mum. Do you hear me?'

Ben nodded. 'Mr Sam?' he asked. 'Please take Mummy on the slide.'

Sam glanced at Sarah. Girls like her would never give him a second look in town, he thought. 'I can't do that, Ben,' he said, shaking his head. 'That's your daddy's job.'

'But I haven't got a daddy.'

Day 3

Watching Ben wolf down his Cheerios on the stained sofa, got Sarah thinking. He was so like his father, Jamie. It was in the way he tilted his head, his wonky grin and wide blue eyes. The best part of five years had passed since she'd last seen Jamie. Where had those years gone?

The resident chef on GMTV chuckled like Fred Flintstone in delight at the trifle he'd whipped together. Realising the time, Sarah reached for the remote control.

'Come on you, we'll be late,' she ordered, zapping the screen to blank.

'I want a trifle, Mummy. I want a trifle!'

'Never mind that,' she called, carrying his bowl through to the kitchen. 'You'll get nothing at this rate.'

At eleven-thirty they finally joined the staggered queue outside the Post Office. Mrs Bailey, who lived opposite, was deep in conversation with that good-for-nothing Frank Casey and 'Crowie' Lowie – two do-gooders that lived on the crescent. Sarah noticed them nudge each other when they saw her approaching. The stigma of being a single parent and the reasons for Ben not being at school, flashed in front of her. They could please themselves, she thought. At least he was safe while he was with her.

Through the aisles of the Late Shop, Ben tugged relentlessly at her sleeve. 'I want to go to the swings.'

Sarah's eyes rested on the glittering chocolate display in front of the tills. She thought about Sam, painting away. Working hard.

'Swings, Mummy,' Ben whined. 'Swings!'

'If you don't behave, you'll go home,' she warned him, unconvinced by her words.

'You mind them potholes!'

Ben charged along the red rutted track, to the side of the dry-cleaners. The high leaves threshed in the poplars. He slowed to take in the water feature at the bottom of Mrs Deakin's garden, before scampering onto the playing field. Sarah's chest tightened as she neared the end of the track. It was the first time in years that she'd felt this way and she paused to compose herself.

Turning from the track, she remained still. Smoke lingered from a smouldering area beneath the climbing frame. There was no sign of Sam's minivan. It was typical, she thought. Nothing changes. Sam couldn't have been gone long and the vandals were at it already.

Ben scurried alongside her as she eased the bag of shopping beside the swings. 'Where's Mr Sam?'

'Shall we go up to the top of the slide and see if we can see him?'

Letting out a high-pitched squeal, Ben made towards the foot of the gleaming red steps.

The gloss paint was dry and the handrails felt smooth. Sam had done a good job. His paint had brought new life to the playground. The colours were brilliant.

From inside the wooden turret, between the top of the steps and the slide, they peered across the landscape. Drying sheets flapped on Swingewood's washing line, the green spire of St James' church almost touched the shifting clouds and the little trucks and cranes edged slowly upon the horizon, above the hum of the opencast project.

A gentle shove and Ben slipped from her arms. In a flash he was back on his feet at the bottom of the slide.

'You have a go Mummy,' he yelled. But after the effort it had taken for her to look glamorous in her new printed dress, she turned back to the steps.

Rummaging in the flimsy carrier bag, the Galaxy chocolate bar she'd bought as a treat for Sam slipped over the back of her hand. She fiddled to break the cellophane from her twenty Richmond's and pivoted to shelter her lighter from the stiffening breeze.

As Ben sprang up the steps to the slide for the fourth time, she cast her mind back to the previous afternoon. Sam had been so patient, wiping the paint from Ben's tiny fingers. When he took him on the slide, Ben's laughter could be heard as far away as the city centre. His energy was boundless. 'Another go! Another go!' he'd screamed. The image of his glowing face as he whizzed into her waiting arms was etched forever. That evening, before she'd put him to bed, he'd asked: 'Is Mr Sam really a spaceman, Mummy?'

Sarah smiled at the Wet Paint sign, taped around the seat of her favourite pink swing. Sam's efficiency was unquestionable. The playground equipment had never looked so good. He was reliable and she believed in him. He mentioned that he'd be finishing today, but she felt disappointed that he'd left so soon.

'Where's Mr Sam?' Ben called, looking at the climbing frame.

'Gone to the bloody moon,' she called, almost laughing at her new-found humour.

'Mummy! Mummy!'

Sarah raised her focus from her unmarked sandals. 'Keep away from there,' she called, making towards the climbing frame.

Burnt remains of cardboard Wet Paint signs lay curled on the blackened paving stones, their silver ashes grinning in the breeze. 'That's the rocket's engines, Ben,' she sighed, attempting to reassure him.

When he turned and reached for her, his hands were a sticky mess, his trousers striped with red paint.

'It's wet!' she snapped, her frustration rising.

Ben started to cry.

'It won't come off.' She grabbed his upper arm and shook him. 'You've ruined them!'

Ben roared and screamed as Sarah marched him home. His crying was relentless. The neighbours were sure to have heard him stomping along the crescent.

'I want Mr Sam,' he cried.

She noticed her thumb marks on his arm and relaxed her grip. They'd be blue tomorrow morning. Slamming Ben's bedroom door behind her, she slumped on the stairs.

The tiny football on the alarm clock, revolved with each second's tick. It was nearly five-thirty. Sarah eased herself on to the edge of the bed. She watched Ben sleeping. His hair ruffled upon the crushed pillow.

She smiled when he stirred. 'There's fish fingers doing in the oven,' she whispered.

His soft eyelashes flickered above his chubby cheeks.

'Hmmm. Fish fingers. And mushy peas.'

Ben sniffled and rubbed his eyes. 'Mummy?' he croaked.

'Yes?'

'Do they have fish fingers and mushy peas in space?'

'Oh yes,' she smiled. 'And lots of other nice things.'

Ben gazed up at her.

'They have perfect skies and magic pies and...'

Clawing the duvet from beneath his chin, Ben's milk teeth glinted, his wonky grin widened. 'Will Mr Sam be having fish fingers for his tea?'

She looked to the side of him, but didn't reply.

'Mr Sam is a nice man.'

She nodded. 'I know he is.'

'Please can we go up to see him soon, Mummy? In the space rocket?'

Trolley Boss
Carolyn Lewis

All the kids call me Bernie, I don't mind that. My mum says every one of my names: Bernard James Robert Phillips, then she asks me a question, 'What am I going to do with you?' When she says that she doesn't say it with a cross face, she sort of sings my name and she always gives me a hug when she comes to Phillips. I think it's because she's got the same last name as me.

She's always very tired, my mum. She says things like, 'Bernard James Robert Phillips, you'll be the death of me.' I don't like it when she says that. I know all about death from when Uncle George and Dad died. That was death. Mum explained it to me, about why they'd died and how they'd both gone to heaven. She said it was a place full of angels and now Dad and Uncle George are up there too and their white wings flutter all the time and, at Christmas, some of the tiny feathers fall and that makes the snow.

I like Christmas. That's when Mum and I go to the big church in town and sing all the carols. *Away in a Manger* is my favourite. I can't always remember the words, but Mum says to do my best and just hum if I'm not sure. People look at me though when I hum. Mum says to ignore them, but they keep on staring.

Last Christmas I bought Mum a big bag of *Pic-n-Mix* from Woolies. I spent ages choosing them: jelly babies, pear drops, jelly beans and some with chocolate on, there were loads of them. Auntie Betty said it was the biggest bag of sweets she'd ever seen. She said she'd have to help Mum eat them all. Auntie Betty also chose a scarf for me to give to Mum as well. She said I could pay her back later, but I forgot.

I earn £8 a week. And it's all mine - I can keep every penny, Mum said I could. She found my job for me. The supermarket where she goes every Friday, she kept on saying it was a disgrace, there were never any trolleys around when people needed them. She said it was criminal the way people left them hanging about in the car park. 'Why can't people take them back for others to use them?' She was always going on about it.

She told the manager, Mr Abrahams, all about me. She didn't say anything to me about getting a job, but she knew I wanted one. She just came home from the supermarket one Friday and said that she'd had a word with the manager. 'I told him that you're trustworthy and reliable. You won't let me down, will you, Bernard?'

She held my hands when she was telling me about the job. She kept on staring into my eyes. 'Now listen to me, Bernard, the manager is a very kind man but he's a very busy man too. He doesn't have the time to check up on what you're doing. It will be your job to bring all the trolleys back from the car park and take them to the area near the door. That's what you do, that's *all* you do. Do you understand me? Are you listening to me?'

She wouldn't let go of my hands until I promised I'd do exactly as I was told.

'This is important, Bernard, promise me.'

I didn't like the way she was staring at me, her eyes didn't blink once. I felt funny when she did that and I tried to move my head away. Mum let go of my hands then and grabbed the sides of my face.

'Look at me, Bernard.' She was using her stern voice, I didn't like it. She was making me nervous. I wriggled and tried to pull her hands away. But she can be really strong sometimes, so in the end I had to look at her.

'You must promise me, Bernard, that you'll do everything you're told. Do you promise?'

I promised, I gave her my word of honour. I even did my special salute, I can still remember it from when I was in the Scouts.

She laughed then and gave me a hug.

'Okay, Bernard James Robert Phillips - how about tea and biscuits to dunk?'

Before I started the job I had to see the manager, Mr Abrahams. Mum took me on a Wednesday morning. She made me put on a clean shirt and she said she didn't think it was a good idea to wear my baseball cap. Mr Abrahams kept us waiting for ages. We were there on time, 11 o'clock, he'd told Mum but even when it was almost 12 o'clock, we were still waiting outside his office.

'Why won't he come? We always have our soup at 12 o'clock. Did you tell him that, Mum?'

Mum didn't answer me, she just shook her head and whispered that I mustn't be too loud.

When Mr Abrahams came out of his office, I put my hand out to shake his. Perhaps he didn't notice because he shook Mum's hand not mine. But he did ask me to sit down when we were in his office.

He asked Mum loads of questions about me: was I strong, could I manage on my own and then he asked, 'Does he need help with getting to the toilets…or anything?'

He looked at me then when he said *toilet* and I wanted to say something to him, to let him know that I wasn't a baby, I could manage, I could go to the toilet on my own, but Mum put her hand out and held mine. That's her signal, we worked it out ages ago and it means that I must keep quiet. 'Even if people say something that makes you upset or hurts you, don't let them see that, just smile.'

So I did, I smiled at Mr Abrahams but even then he wasn't looking at me, he was looking at Mum. 'Bernard can cope perfectly well on his own, he won't need any help at all.' Mum sat up as she spoke, her back was really straight and she wasn't smiling any more. Mr Abrahams looked at me, but it was a really quick look so I don't think he saw me smiling at him.

'You understand, Mrs Phillips that neither I nor my staff have got time to spare for, well, for helping Bernard. He'll have to manage on his own.'

He hadn't heard Mum, hadn't heard her say that I could manage all by myself. I tried to move, I wanted to tell him again but Mum's hands were holding mine so tight she was hurting me and I knew she wanted me to sit still and not say a word, so I didn't.

Then Mum tugged at my arm when Mr Abrahams stood up and we both stood as he opened the door of his office.

Mum sighed, she does that sometimes when people have upset her and she held my hand again when we were outside the office. 'Do you understand, Bernard? Do you know what you've got to do? A few hours a day, collecting the trolleys? Do you think you can manage that?'

I nodded at her, she laughed and said that if I nodded any harder, my head would fall off. I laughed then and we walked out of the supermarket. Mum told me to stand still and wait for her by the door and she went back in again. When she came out she was holding two Mars bars.

'One for you, Bernard James Robert Phillips and one for me.'

I told her that I'd keep mine for later or I wouldn't eat my lunch. She gave me a hug and said I'd be the death of her.

I was so excited the night before I started my job. Mum said I was even worse than the night before my birthday. My birthday's in May. Each year she says I must learn to act like an adult, every time my birthday comes around she says it and I'm forty-four now. Mum says I'm like a bull, charging around after things. She says she didn't believe all that nonsense about star signs before I was born but she does now.

She bought me a new pair of trousers when I started working at the supermarket, 'I want you to look smart, you're doing an important job. You're in charge, you're the boss of the supermarket trolleys. Mr Abrahams is *your* boss but you're the boss of all those trolleys.'

I know a lot of the people who shop at the supermarket: there's Mr and Mrs Cummings, they live opposite the library and there's Mrs Armstrong, she works in the Post Office and that woman Mum doesn't like, the one with the twins, Julie and Katie. Everyone knows about my job and they tell me what a difference I'm making. 'A pleasure to do my shopping now,' Mr Cummings said that to me. When I told Mum what he'd said she had tears in her eyes. She said she didn't but I could see them.

It's hard work, my job. There's a lot of standing and watching. Some people just push their trolleys away after they're finished with them. They send them into the sides of other cars so that's why I watch. Sometimes I walk behind people as they leave the supermarket and I watch them to see that they don't just leave them or push them against cars. They mustn't do that and it's my job to see that the trolleys aren't damaged. People think that trolleys aren't important, but they are. I'm in charge of them. I'm their boss.

I took my pay envelope home to show Mum. The big, fat girl

who works in the office came out to the car park. She gave me the envelope, it had my name on it: Bernard Phillips. I told her that I had other names as well, Bernard, James, Robert Phillips. I told her but she wasn't listening. She kept looking over her shoulder all the time, some of the other girls in the supermarket were watching her.

Mum asked why I hadn't opened my envelope, 'It's got your name on it, it's yours, you've earned it.' She said she'd put the money in the Post Office for me and she gave me a hug. 'I'm so proud of you, Bernard, you're doing a very good job.'

I like my job, being in charge of the trolleys. I didn't like it when people left plastic bags in them or orange peel or crisp packets. They shouldn't do that, it's not nice. I got some carrier bags from the supermarket and put all the rubbish in them. Mr Abrahams came out once to see me. He saw me putting rubbish in the bags and he said I was doing a good job. He gave me a badge too, it had my name on it, *Bernard* written in red letters. He said I should wear it on my jumper. I told him that I'd got other names, 'Bernard James, Robert Phillips - they're all my names.'

'Don't think the badge is big enough for that, Bernard.' Mr Abrahams was in a hurry, Mum keeps telling me that he's a busy man.

'Everything all right, Bernard? Got any problems?' He'd started to walk away without waiting for me to answer him.

'No, no problems, I can manage. I like looking after the trolleys.' I wanted him to know that. I wanted him to look at my trolleys, see how clean they were, see how I kept them parked in the proper place.

But Mr Abrahams walked off, he just said 'Good, that's good.' And he didn't even look at the trolleys.

Some lads started to come into the car park. It was all right at first, they gave me crisps and chocolate. Some of them smoke too. I told them it was a bad thing, you can get cancer, but they laughed at me. They said they didn't care, they said I shouldn't let things like that worry me.

They started to come every day, even when they should have been in school. They brought big bottles of cider and, when they'd drunk it all, they left the empty bottles in the trolleys. They started pushing the trolleys up and down the car park, they even started riding in them and shouting at other people. I told them not to do that, I said I was in charge of the trolleys and they were making a mess of them. I didn't like it.

One of them, the one called Carl, tried to pull my badge off my jumper. I said it was mine, I said Mr Abrahams had given it to me for being in charge of the trolleys.

Carl asked me why my name was Bernard. 'Did your mother call you that after one of those big, slobbering dogs?'

I didn't know what he meant. 'No, I'm called Bernard after my Dad. He died, he's in heaven now.'

'Yeah, bet he is, must have been the shock after seeing you…'

Carl and his friends came in every day. They'd even be there at night. I knew that because I could see that the trolleys had been moved when I got to work in the morning. I didn't know what to do. I told Mum and she said that I was only there to tidy up the trolleys, nothing else. 'Just do what you're paid for, don't get involved, Bernard.'

Carl and his gang were in the car park last week. There were a lot of them and they'd been drinking, they dropped cans of beer and bottles of cider everywhere. One of them had been sick, it was all over the seat of one of the trolleys. I told Carl that they mustn't do that, it was my job to look after the trolleys.

I pushed the trolleys back to the right place. I got a cloth to clean the sick up. Carl and his gang walked behind me, they were all laughing. I told them it wasn't funny, I told them that they mustn't come to the car park again if they didn't look after the trolleys. They pulled faces and called me names. *Barmy Bernard, Bollocks to Bernard, Bernard's a bugger.*

They wouldn't stop, they shouted at me all the time, *Barmy Bernard.*

Everyone was looking at me, girls from the supermarket were pointing, staring out through the big windows. Then Mr Abrahams came out, he was walking really fast. Carl and his gang ran away when they saw him.

'Bernard, what's going on? Are you all right, did they hurt you?' Mr Abrahams's face was all red and his hair was sticking up.

I told him I was okay, I told him that I'd clean up the trolleys. I said it wasn't my fault. I didn't make the mess, 'I look after the trolleys, I'm in charge of them.'

'Yes, okay, that's okay.' He walked back to his office and I saw him talking to one of the girls by the door of the supermarket. They just stood there, looking at me. I thought they were cross about the mess in the trolleys. I cleaned it all up, every bit of sick. But it wasn't my fault.

Mr Abrahams phoned Mum last night. She was in our hall and all I could hear her say was, 'But that's not fair, it wasn't his fault, that's not fair…'

When she finished talking Mum came back into the room. She had two red patches on her cheeks. She sat down on the couch next to me and held my hands.

'Listen to me, Bernard. You can't go to the supermarket any more. Mr Abrahams says he doesn't want any trouble. He knows it's not your fault, but he still says you can't look after the trolleys any longer. Do you understand?'

'No! I did a good job, I'm in charge of the trolleys. Those boys made the mess, I didn't. I look after the trolleys, I didn't make them dirty.'

Mum was holding my hands really tight. 'I know, son, I'm sorry.'

I went to the supermarket this morning. There were two big blokes there, they were just standing around. They were wearing blue jumpers, they didn't have name badges though, they had the word *Security* written on the back of their jumpers. I didn't go in to the car park, I only stood by the trolley park.

One of the blokes told me to move away and I shook my head. Then the other one said, 'Piss off, you're scaring the customers.'

I'm not, I wouldn't do that. I only want to watch people, I only want to see that they put the trolleys away properly. I'm in charge of them.

Rich Tea And Custard Creams

Penny Aldred

Monday

7.50am. You take the sandwiches from the fridge. Sliced ham from yesterday, with French mustard, in granary bread, an apple, a cereal bar. Shout upstairs, 'Bye pet, have a nice day,' out the front door, down the path, turn right.

It's a ten-minute walk to the station. You arrive at the platform with three minutes to spare.

8.12am. The train to Victoria pulls out.

You get off, walk past Urbis, down between Marks and Spencer's and Harvey Nicks, reach Albert Square and up the stairs into the town hall. Shallow stairs, long strides. Along corridors, round corners, into your office.

'Morning, George.'

'Morning, Tom.'

Put your briefcase on your desk, open it, take out your lunch box, cross the carpet to the fridge, put the sandwiches on the shelf, second shelf, left hand side at the front, back to your desk, sit down, switch on the computer, check your emails.

Tuesday

7.50am. You take sandwiches from the fridge. Egg mayonnaise, homemade, that Sandra made last night, in white bread, a banana, a cereal bar. Shout upstairs, 'Bye pet, have a nice day,' out the front door, down the path, turn right.

8.14am. The train to Victoria pulls out.

You're sitting opposite the same man as yesterday. You've sat opposite him most mornings for the last seven years. Not every morning because sometimes someone else gets his seat, sometimes someone else gets your seat. Sometimes he's on holiday, and then when he reappears, he's relaxed for a few days, a week or two. You could have spoken to him, once upon a time, but now it's not possible, too much time has gone sitting opposite each other and not speaking. You've also seen him at work, in the canteen. When Sandra was in hospital for a week you ate there, and then when she stayed with her mum the day after her dad died, you ate there too. You saw him, the man from the train, eating his lunch, a book propped up against the sauce bottles. You looked away and sat at the far end, so he didn't wonder if you'd seen him and ignored him. You don't know where in the town hall he works.

Most mornings he has a book. Usually a travel book. This last week he's been reading a book about climbing. The cover has a photo of mountains, pink sky, a celebrity in the foreground.

He's ten, fifteen years older than you, similar suit, white shirts where you favour blue, and sometimes green. You feel as if you know him. Last winter he wasn't on the train for three weeks. When he reappeared he hadn't the hint of a tan. He was pale, withdrawn. His shirts had lost their pristine sharpness, his shoes were a little dusty. But after a month or so his face had its working mask on, as though nothing had changed, though you noticed the shirts were never quite so smart, the collars not quite so straight.

8.27am. You get off. It's raining. Put up your umbrella, walk past Urbis, between Marks and Spencer's and Harvey Nicks, reach Albert Square and up the stairs to the town hall. Shallow stairs, long strides. Along corridors, round corners, into your office.

'Morning George.'

'Morning Tom.'

Wednesday

7.50am. You take sandwiches from the fridge. Cheddar cheese and Branston pickle. Shout upstairs…well, you get the picture. It's your life.

Thursday

Tuna sandwiches in your briefcase, you get off the 8.12 train, walk past Urbis.

Then you skirt round the front of Marks and Spencer's, sit on one of the stone tiered benches, look up at the television screen, so large that the image is fuzzy, you can see each square divided from its neighbours. You put your briefcase on your knees, unfasten the catch and slide out a plastic wallet.

In your hands you hold photographs, A4, black and white, some shiny, sharp, others grainy, the images misty. They're the city at night, or rather, in the evening, when the workers have left and the streets belong to a different population.

There's a woman crouched in a doorway, her Asda shopping trolley piled high with carrier bags, blankets draped over the top. In another a man, young, a suit, leans against a lamppost, reading a paperback under the street lamp. Another and there's mist rising from the canal, lovers gazing from a bridge into the water below.

These pictures have angles, sharpness, vertical lines echoing vertical lines, with the softness or chaos of lives on top. The city is there, never changing, built to stay the same so you always know where you are.

With the photos there's a leaflet, an application form for a post as city photographer. A year capturing the urban landscape, decay and regeneration, plus a course at the university. The deadline's today. Midday.

You slip the photographs, the form, back into the wallet, put it back into your briefcase, get up and head down Cross Street.

Upstairs into the office.

'Morning George, your train late today?'

'Morning Tom.'

You sit at your desk, switch on the computer, listen to it booting up, starting your day. You stare through the window at the pigeons on the roof opposite.

Check your emails.

Check your in-tray.

Anything in your diary?

Check your emails.

10.15am. You hear the tea-trolley down the corridor. It rattles into your office, the wheels suddenly silenced on the carpet.

You take the photographs out, spread them over your desk. You look at the lines, the sharpness, the clear definitions, the metal and concrete, framing and contrasting with the roundness of living.

Teresa brings your tea over. Two biscuits in the saucer; one custard cream, one rich tea.

'Interesting.'

You turn to Teresa.

'You like them?'

'Yes.' She concentrates. 'Yes.' She describes what she sees, the sharp-edged city and the soft fuzzy people, living and working there. She sees exactly what you hoped to capture.

Teresa's about your age, just a couple of years younger. In fact she was in the same year at school as Sandra.

You found this out when you and Sandra were taking a walk along the tow path and you met Teresa. It was a Sunday morning, early. You'd persuaded Sandra to go into the city, to see it in its stillness and monochrome, before the day trippers were out, loud and brash enjoying their leisure time in their leisure clothes.

Teresa was painting, her easel blocking the path. There was no way you could avoid her. You stopped, said hello, introduced Sandra and Teresa and discovered that they knew each other. They had a brief conversation about who they were still in touch with, who was married, who had babies.

Then you felt you couldn't avoid looking at what she was doing. You and Sandra stood behind her, looking over her shoulder. Nervous in case what you saw wasn't very good, in case you couldn't find anything to say. Would 'very nice' do?

But you saw that she'd captured something of the derelict mill opposite, something about it, coltsfoot growing on window sills, glass broken, the decay of the past. It wasn't an exact representation, but you recognised some feeling in the picture. You were mightily impressed. And said so.

'Don't you be like that with me, Georgie,' she'd said.

Sandra shifted beside you, let go of your hand.

'Just because I bring you tea and biscuits in the morning, remember there's more to me than that. More to my life than that.'

'I didn't mean to be offensive,' you said. 'It's just that you've got an eye. And good technique.'

'Thanks. It didn't just happen you know. I've worked hard over the years, college and everything.'

Sandra looked at her watch.

'Well, I'd best get on with my painting, nice to see you,' said Teresa.

As you walked away, Sandra told you that Teresa was one of the bad set, skipping lessons, never handing her homework in on time.

'No wonder she's pushing a tea trolley in the council offices,' she said.

You didn't respond. You were thinking about Teresa's picture, how she'd got the light in the sky, the water, the broken glass.

But after that you and Teresa talked about her painting. She told you about exhibitions with her painting group, then a restaurant that wanted half a dozen of her paintings on the walls, for sale, and how she'd got a couple of commissions from that. That she was beginning to hope that soon she could paint full-time.

You never told her about your hobby.

So she's surprised now to discover that you take photographs, capture images.

'What's this?' she picks up the leaflet. 'Better get your skates on Georgie boy.'

Teresa goes back to her trolley, takes tea, coffee, biscuits to your colleagues. Leaves the office.

You turn to the back of your diary and add to the running total of biscuits you've eaten at that desk. Two a day for the last eighteen years, starting with ginger and digestive, after seven years giving up ginger for rich tea, and then two years later swapping digestives for custard creams. You subtract two from the total of biscuits (variety as yet undecided) to be eaten before retirement.

10.45am. Andrew Morrison, your line-manager comes in, asks if you can spare him a few minutes. You go into his office. You hear as he talks about the work you've done this last few months, what the department's plans are for the next few. How you will fit in.

You look at the ridges on the roof, the lines of tiles, the guttering. A pigeon lands, totters across the tiles. You wonder if it was one that you saw earlier.

'So George. What do you think?'

You've not heard the specifics, but you've got the gist. Enough to say that you are up for it, that it will be a challenge but isn't that what life, work, is all about. They can count on you.

11.30am. Back at your desk.

You check your emails.

The morning post has been delivered, check your in-tray to see what has arrived. You take out a report, two pages of something. Put it on the desk, remove the paper clip in the top left corner, put the clip in the pot you keep for paper clips.

Read the report.

Take a paper clip from the pot, attach it to the top left hand corner.

Put the report in your in-tray.

11.40am. Teresa appears.

'Hi Georgie.'

'Hello.'

'So. Thought I'd check on you. Still here? Are you going? Only twenty minutes left?'

'No. I've decided no. It's more of a hobby. And there's interesting things happening here. At work.'

Teresa raises her eyebrows.

'It was just a dream. You know.'

'No, I don't know. Dreams can happen.'

Teresa walks out. As she goes through the door she calls out, 'I'd never got you down as a quitter Georgie. But then, you can't tell much about a man from the biscuits he eats, can you?'

You hear her down the corridor. She must be singing loud because you hear, 'If you don't have a dream…how you gonna have a dream come true?'

A door opens and someone shouts, 'Keep your voice down will you? We've an important meeting in here.'

That does it. You open the drawer, snatch the folder, rush out of the door.

'I'm taking an early lunch. Back in an hour.'

And you're out, speeding along the corridor, taking the stairs two at a time till you reach the bottom and fear that you'll fall over, you're going so fast.

Out into Albert Square and a deep breath, the air right down into your lungs. Skirt round the town hall, you can see the gallery at the far end of the street and there's still ten minutes. Thank you Teresa.

And then Teresa's there, in front of you, walking away from you towards the bus stop.

For a moment you're going to tap her on the shoulder, give her a thumbs up sign, say thank you. For a moment you're going to put your arm round her shoulder and put a huge, fat kiss on her cheek. You're going to take both her hands in yours and spin her round in the street and sing.

Then you see her black tights, a ladder running from her left ankle, heading north to her knee. You see her heels, worn on the outside so her feet kind of splay out. Her coat is bobbled and the hem dips.

You hear your mother, boasting how proud she is that you have a job in an office, a job where you can wear a suit, a tie, your hands are clean at the end of the day. You see yourself in a few years' time, knocking at the town hall door, standing there in the same suit, shiny with age, asking for your job back. You see Sandra, with a part-time cleaning job, worn and tired. You see her darning your socks, sewing patches on the elbows of your jackets. She's walking down the garden path, dragging a suitcase, leaving you. You think of the man on the train, his collar's just not quite right. And then your father is telling of your selfishness, your irresponsibility. No savings and oh god, he has seen the gap in your pension contributions.

You carry on, past a sandwich shop, its queue out the door.

Ahead there's a bank, another bank, a travel agent's. You keep a distance behind Teresa, but she stops at the travel agent's, talks to someone, a man looking in the window. It's the man from the train.

There's no escaping and Teresa sees you.

'Georgie, you going after all? Good on you. This is Frank. Georgie. You two met? Georgie's in corporate procurement. Frankie's in strategic management. You live out the same way too.'

She stops and you both look at her. She looks at her watch.

'Got to dash, bus to catch. Pictures to paint.' She's walking away from you both, giving a wave.

The man on the train, Frank, kind-of smiles, nods.

'A holiday? Climbing a mountain?' you say, pointing to the book tucked under his arm.

'God no. Two weeks rest, that's what I want. Enough hassle at work.'

He's looking in the window, at the cards pinned up, the bargains, the last-minute deals.

'No point in working all year and then sweating all holiday. Take life easy when you can, that's what I say.'

'Right, hope you find what you're looking for.' You walk on. Past a building society, another sandwich shop, another queue.

The gallery's across the road. There's a poster on the railings advertising the photography competition, with a diagonal strip of paper across it. 'Deadline – Noon' is written in felt-tip pen. There's faces in the two 'o's, with crying eyes and mouths turned down at the sides.

You think of Teresa's poor sad shoes, with worn down heels.

You turn left, down side streets until you reach the stone seats outside Marks and Spencer's.

The folder's on your knee. You slide out the top photograph. It's a man looking in a rubbish bin, his hand in a plastic bag, taking something out, something too far away for the camera to see. The camera has caught the pleasure on his face. You put the photograph back.

You sit there and watch the midday news.

The Hand That Whirls The Water

Alexandra Fox

The ring is rinsed of warm blood with cold water, and put into the daughter's hand.

It is made of platinum, worn thin, a small circle chased with a whispered tracery of entwining stems, its inscription long effaced by the rub of flesh. They must have tugged it from its deep valley on her mother's unprotesting finger, forced it over the sink-swollen knuckle, torn it from the suck of her skin, ungloving the fat white lady.

They place it in the centre of the daughter's palm, and she says, 'No. Put it back. She never took it off in fifty years. It still has the blessing inside.' So they push it back down the finger, smoothing wrinkles out of loose, torn skin.

The daughter, Alison, takes the gold-coloured watch and loose change and drops them into her mother's handbag, crammed with unfinished knitting and a stack of birthday cards, addressed, stamped, dated through the year, grave-sent greetings, unstoned cherries to crack unsuspecting teeth.

She examines her mother, seeing that all things are done decently and in order, that her eyes and mouth are closed, that the sheet is drawn up to her neck and down over her horny toenails, draping the bag of trickled urine. Then she calls her father in.

The silent soft-eyed nurse has moved the chairs away as she goes about her business, tidying, closing, wiping. Alison and her father sat there earlier, on either side of the bed. The chairs were low and hard, and she craned her neck like a child at a tea-table counting the candles on a cake. They each had the gift of a hand to cosset, a puppet hand, floppy, centre-strung with tapped wires, a hand to put aside when dealing with a lunch-time sandwich, cup and saucer. The daughter led the conversation, speaking over the body, brightly reminiscing, telling tales of her childhood, schooldays, old told stories remembered only by the telling.

As the spaces between the phlegm-cracked breaths grew longer, darker, the windows turned to mirrors; she spoke of weddings, of grandchildren, their graduations, qualifications, ambitions. She listed a legacy, worthwhile, world-spanning.

The silences stretched across the bed.

The father stood, kicked back his chair with a grating squeal across the streaked vinyl floor. Alison flinched. Her mother lay unmoving.

'I can't stay here, waiting for her to go. Tell me when it's over.'

His elbow-cornered body buffered her approach, her comfort.

The daughter stood by her mother's head, cradling it in the scoop of her fingers, smoothing grease-flat hair against pink scalp with both thumbs. She spoke repetitive, hypnotic words of love and soft, shared memories, and as she spoke she heard herself, and thought, I'm standing at my mother's deathbed and I'm stroking her hair, I'm talking to her, I'm giving her comfort. Mine are the last words she will hear. She stored up these thoughts, these words, the feel of slowing circulation with a rare, quiet importance. She looked close into the insipid vacancy of blue eyes, once hazel. She watched for the last breath, studying the bubbling mouth, timing the shudder-judder birth-death contractions. Still she spoke on and on, spilling loving words, pouring prayers by rote, not noticing the waves of repetition.

One breath was longer, deeper, dying away. The daughter listened for a rattle, watched for a slumping, a smallness, any alteration to show the passing of a soul, a change she could later describe as seeing death. She looked through the window for a change in the light, an owl, a black bird flying away.

Five minutes passed; she turned to call the nurse.

And then she died again. A long-drawn breath, gathering in the air, holding in the sigh, not letting go.

This death was final, unmistakeable, uncaressed, unspoken to, behind her daughter's back.

* * *

She wraps soft arms around her father, a big man. The stiffness of his body is belied by the formless wetness welling in the troughs of his eyelids, the helpless wobble of loose lips. His skin mottles with embarrassment. There is no give in him.

'Leave me alone with her for a few minutes.'

'I'll wait outside. Come when you need me.'

She sits on a concrete bench. Security lights flash on and off with dawn-not-dawn, flooding white across washed grey. A pot is planted with cigarette gravestones in ash-strewn sand.

She flips open her phone. The numbers are pre-programmed.

'Peter, I'm at the hospital. I'm afraid I've got bad news... Stephen, I'm so sorry to wake you...'

It is four o'clock in the morning. Their mother was expected to die. She will still be dead at seven.

The automatic doors open and shut for a wraith-like eddy of dead leaves. Air is exchanged. Outside is the rich mulch odour of decay.

The doors slide open again for her father. He walks slowly, as though the small of his back pains him with stiffness from the long sitting. His daily handkerchief is tight within his hand, its ironed folds crumpled round the wetness of its core.

Driving to the bungalow she checks each thought, unvoiced. He snuffles.

She thinks about the slackness of her mother's mouth and how the nurses closed it, that she'll never let her own toenails turn yellow, her father's full laundry basket, of hymns, hassocks, black bin bags, of don't it make your brown eyes blue, that the only spare bed is her mother's, the thin smell of urine, how skin turns finger-dipping soft like dough when the heart stops pumping.

Outside the house she leans across her father's lap, unfastens the child-lock, snaps his seatbelt open, and he says, 'Don't come in, Alison, not now. I need a bit of time by myself.'

It is half-past-four; she has no luggage, toothbrush, hotel room. He will need her in the morning to make the arrangements. She drives a few yards down the road and parks under the grey skeleton of a silver-birch tree.

The car is a small Fiat. The front seats cannot recline further than the back seats will permit. It is cold without a blanket, so she curls her knees up on the seat and wraps her arms around herself, crossing her chest, holding in her own warmth. She huddles in exquisite pillowless discomfort, the gearstick pressing into the small of her back, rigid, irritating, inescapable.

In the not-quite-dawn her father's windows glow yellow. She sees him step stiffly through the living room, fade into the darkness of the hall, walk across the kitchen, turn, reverse, walk, pace, turn, walk, fade and her dry eyes droop.

* * *

Driving home up the motorway, Baremboim plays the Pathètique. She switches to Radio Two.

The roughness of unbrushed teeth annoys her tongue.

She thinks about catfood, the rush hour, bins not put out for the dustmen, superglue, data entry, the chicken in the freezer that would take eight hours to thaw for supper, Mastercard, a teenage diary entry about blowjobs that she wishes she hadn't read, that tiredness kills take a break. Her thoughts turn, reverse, pace and she yawns with air hunger and feels her dry eyes itch and droop.

She stops at a service station and orders a large white Americano with an extra shot. It comes in a cardboard cup, tall as a witch's hat. She drinks half of it, perching at a round steel drum-table on a one-legged stool, high, disconnected, like a fairground ride about to whirl vertiginously. The coffee scalds her mouth, a blistered pain that she does not yet feel.

The wife, Alison, drives for two more hours, sipping cold coffee through a sharp plastic lid.

Spitting drizzle turns to grey persistent rain.

Serial speed cameras do not flash.

* * *

She lives at number twenty-five, different from its neighbours, identical to numbers fifteen and twenty, goldfish individuality. The house exhales balti breath. The cartons lie on the curry-encrusted tablecloth, among forks, plates, cereal bowls, crusts of dry toast. The dishwasher is still full, but the vases are empty; the notepad stands blank on the hall chest.

A shirtsleeve dangles through the banisters. She drags herself upstairs. Katie's room is the antithesis of the painted perfection that will have left for college that morning; she shuts that door. She gathers laundry, holding socks, pants, sweat-soaked shirts against herself.

Downstairs she fills the washing machine, stacks, rinses, puts away crockery, cutlery, pans. Systematically she cleans her kitchen, her househeart place.

She peels papery skin from shallots, chops mushrooms, drizzles carnaroli rice with olive oil. She steeps black porcini corpses in old wine. Black. Funeral hats, skirts, jackets, suitable shoes, fat hips, buttons, laddered tights, dandruff, ties, same-day-cleaners.

* * *

At supper, the wife, Alison, sits across the table from her husband.

In front of her is a dish of risotto, the rice ash-strewn with parmesan, studded with mushroom pieces. She slices garlic bread, dresses a salad of pallid chicory leaves. She sips Frascati; he drinks a dense, drying Barolo.

He asks cautiously about her mother's passing. Was it very harrowing, did she wake up at all, say any last words?

'No. It was peaceful. I was with her at the end. I talked to her, stroked her as she died, but I don't think she knew I was there. I hope she did.'

He asks about the traffic, the journey home, the week ahead, compassionate paid leave from her work, the funeral arrangements.

'The funeral's on Tuesday. She'd already made all the plans herself, years ago…just the crematorium, Father John taking the service, family only, no gravestone.'

'Tuesday. This Tuesday? Yes of course this Tuesday. Silly question. That could be tricky. I'll have to cancel meetings.'

She takes a mouthful of bread. It dries in her mouth, unswallowable. She gulps wine and forces it down into her stomach as a hard lump.

'It's at eleven.'

'Is Katie coming?'

'No. Katie's at the Clothes Show. Her tutor group is going that day, and she doesn't want to go with another set. She says that Granny would understand.'

'She's out tonight?'

'Yes, at a gig. That's why she isn't eating with us.'

Frascati should be light, delicate, flowery on the tongue. This bottle must be old; it's sour.

Katie had rushed in off the bus, flawlessly, wantonly disordered, bed-hair, distressed jeans, eyes smudged grey with shadow, every feature placed immaculately for effect.

The mother, Alison, took her into the enclosing circle of her arms, held her as she sobbed that she couldn't bear it. How would they manage without Granny? She'd miss her so much. Was the journey bad? When did you get back, Mum? Did you have time to pick those films up from the chemists? When is the funeral? No, she can't go down all that way on Tuesday. Anyway, she'd cry. She'd be bound to cry, it's so sad, her Granny dying. She'd cry and embarrass everybody. Would you think I was terrible, Mum, if I went out tonight? I'm sure you just want to be quiet. It's all so sad. There's this gig, you see.

'Are your brothers going?' Her husband is speaking.

'Where?'

'To the funeral.'

'Peter and Stephen are, with Mandy, and Anna if she can get a babysitter. Phil can't get a flight at this short notice, not one he can afford. I must remember to order flowers for him. I'll organize the flowers tomorrow, and get started on the food.'

'Food?'

'For the neighbours, back at the house after the service. I said I'd do some sausage rolls, sandwiches, a cake. The boys are bringing sherry.'

'You'll be exhausted. Look, you must be tired out now. Why not go up, have a bath, an early night? Leave the clearing away. It can wait until the morning.'

The wife wakes.

Her head had slumped its weight into the hollow of her pillow, cradled in exquisite, immediate oblivion by its soft support.

The bed is hot. Her husband lies beside her. He is unshowered, pores exuding garlic and wine.

His erection presses against the small of her back, rigid, irritating, inescapable. She catches her sigh between clenched teeth and rolls over.

His weight is taken on his arms, on either side of her body, scarcely touching, joined at the hip. She turns her face away from his heavy winebreath, eyes closed. She kneads his buttocks in the scoop of her hands, hurrying his uneven thrusts. Her knees are too heavy to lift.

She thinks of wreaths, a dense ivy wreath with a dark hole in the middle, of stalks wrapped dripping in a cellophane sheath, bamboo, deep-pink-centred orchids, buttonhole carnations with blue-dyed edges, the smell of salt-caked feathered grasses, decaying chrysanthemums drooping in a bucket by a grave. She sleeps.

* * *

The daughter, Alison, wipes white from her hands across her arse-draping sweater. She changes the CD, sliding out Simon and Garfunkel, replacing them with the Fauré Requiem. She needs to choose funeral music to blanket the shadowless sound of silence, to muffle the turning wheels.

The kitchen table is dusted with flour. To the first notes of the introit she rolls out a rectangle of dough, scores it into thirds, and chequers it with dabs of butter. She folds it in upon itself, sealing the edges with frigid water, gives it a quarter-turn clockwise and rolls again.

She thinks of a solo boy chorister, unbroken voice wobbling with nerves, singing to her through the radio from the chapel of Kings College on Christmas Eve, year upon year, as she and her mother and her mother before her folded, enfolded, wrapped and turned their puff pastry clockwise, rolled it out and folded it again.

She takes a fruit cake from the bottom oven, and replaces it with a casserole.

* * *

Monday evening, and Alison, the daughter, sits at her father's table. She has brought him a cottage pie, and he has managed to eat just a little while she watches him. She will leave the rest on the side in the kitchen, hoping that snacked mouthfuls will not be flavoured by the self-consciousness of grief.

His fridge is stacked with temporary Tupperware; his freezer is full.

'You're a good daughter. I couldn't manage all this on my own.'

'I promised Mum I'd come, to sort her things out, to make sure that you're all right, that you can manage.'

'I don't know what I'm going to do without her. What's going to happen to me?'

'Don't think about it now, Dad. Let's just get through tomorrow; that'll be hard enough. Don't make any decisions yet.'

There is dried egg between the tines of her fork. Every glass is smeared. The teacups are stained with brown tree-rings. She switches on the immersion heater, and sits her father down to watch the news.

She empties the cutlery drawer into the sink, shakes the crumbs out of the window.

Yesterday, she had suggested to her husband that they travel down the evening before the funeral, stay overnight in a hotel. Safer, in case of traffic, she'd said. They were to follow the hearse, to leave the house half-an-hour early. It was important that they weren't late. And anyway, she had promised her mother that she'd sort her wardrobe out herself – clothes to keep, to give to Oxfam, to throw away.

The water isn't hot yet. She pours a boiling kettle into the sink, adds detergent, watches the bubbles swirl, a hint of oily rainbow lustre in the dim light.

He'd told her that he had to play bridge. He couldn't let his partner down.

She tips the bowl from side to side, helping the heat work upon the grease, stripping it. She adds cold water, just enough that her hands can bear it, watches her white skin turn red. She loosens encrustations with a brush, polishes the old silver with a soft cloth till it glows and reflects.

She packed the car that morning, with baking and her good black coat and skirt. She'd filled the cat's bowl with dried food, left a meal in the fridge with heating instructions, an envelope for Katie with cash for taxis, buses, emergencies. Her husband's suit was hung on the front of the wardrobe, pressed and brushed, a white shirt inside the jacket, black tie draped around the hanger. She'd polished his shoes.

She covers the table with white linen and fans the gleaming knives across one corner, folds paper napkins, arranges asters and beech leaves in a vase. She pours another kettleful of boiling water, starts washing glasses. The water from the tap is hot enough for rinsing now. The hidden facets of Waterford lead crystal re-emerge with gleaming iridescence.

* * *

It is late, silent but for the slow tick of an unseen clock.

The daughter, Alison, sits cross-legged on her mother's bed. She tucks her short, fair hair behind her ears. The envelope is brown manilla, but it needs to be asbestos to contain the heat inside.

The room is piled with bags, black plastic bin-bags tipping with clothes, patent leather handbags, the medibag full of stoma patches, tailored to the loathed excrescence on her side. Hangered clothes are heaped on the bed, pleated grey skirts, navy jackets, white blouses. Two hats lie on top of the wardrobe like a thespian mask, one black, small crowned for funerals, the other her wedding hat, creamy white, saucer-shaped. Flat shoes, fat shoes.

The envelope was taped to the back of the cupboard, blank except for a single sentence handwritten across the flap.

'Tread softly, for you tread upon my dreams.'

The daughter is intrigued, uneasy. She thinks of a bee box, of photographs of flesh, of lovers' letters, adultery, birth certificates, adoption, secret scalpels of silver-bright destruction ripping lives apart.

She finds white pages jewelled by rainbow prisms.

The first page is a sonnet, simple and tender, about a baby's little milky-mouth, joy unconstrained by the rigid form, the couplet turning to fear for the future. There are several more experiments with verse forms, poignant, domestic, growing in confidence, ready to leap.

Then she leaps, and blood seeps. Free verse overflows with purple frustrated passion, gothic tales of visceral gore, eroticism in flamingo pink, apricot afternoons of languorous loving, comedies of manners, convoluted, clever language – foul and funny, illusion, allusion, quotation, Mediterranean seas, powder-paint skies – life under white flat roofs where the staircase leads only to love on top amid the reinforcing rods, stream of consciousness meandering through greening woods and seasons, ever slapshot emotions, intertwining limbs, flesh. The words are focussed through a lens of frustration. Most of all there are stories, acerbic, incisive, of a shadow-man who drives away her friends with sarcasm, who doesn't know how, where, when to touch, of his secret scornful cruelties and base humiliations. It is an unstoppable spillage from arms that have encircled, that have held, held on, and can contain no longer.

There is so much bitterness and abnegation. This little dumpy wife-mother, blonde hair chopped as short as her daughter's, lonely, housebound, unconsidered, had lived this life, this rich life below the surface, this brilliance, this whirlwind wonder-rush of images, imagination, inundation. She had lived. It's just that nobody had noticed.

* * *

Alison waits inside the door of the crematorium's chapel. She's not wearing the black hat, but is not quite brave enough to put on the white flying saucer.

She greets her brothers and her sisters-in-law, kissing cheeks lightly, patting shoulders, murmuring shared condolences, always listening for the sound of a car.

The coffin is of simple oak. It looms.

She had ordered the flowers from home, studying the arrangements on a computer screen, tapping suitable messages for the sympathy cards.

There was a spray of proteas, red amaranthus and orchids from the Australian son, a wreath of dahlias, chrysanthemums and ivy from the rest, in mellow autumnal colours once loved. Her father's flowers were the most difficult.

'But how can I choose for you, Dad? What did she like?'

'She loved her garden. She worked hard in it – green fingers.'

'Did you ever buy her flowers?'

'I bought her roses once, six red roses for Valentine's Day when we were courting. I had to walk to work for a week because I spent my bus fare on them.'

So it's six red roses, backed with a spray of gypsophylia, tied with natural raffia. She'd asked for them not to be wrapped in cellophane, to lie directly on the wood. She doesn't regret her choice even now; those Valentine roses were from a time before the dreams were trodden.

Ashkenasy comes to the end of the second movement of the Pathètique, played softly while the family do not speak. Alison changes the CD for another from the same case, turns up the volume.

It is three minutes before eleven. No car.

Father John will be crossing his stole across his breast. He will take this hard despite his faith, a farewell to a long-time friend. When he heard her confession, was it just the colourless sins, or did she tell him of her inner life? Had he been told of apricot afternoons, blue passion on the flat roofs of Corfu villages, deep longings for the bloody disembowelling of the husband shackled to her by his Church? Was he shocked, aroused, delighted? Did he offer absolution for the imagination?

Eleven o'clock. The Apassionata sonata pours joyfully from the sound system.

Alison wraps her arms around herself. She shivers in the crematorium's dry heat. She yearns.

She goes to the coffin, rearranges the flowers. She slips the gold band from her finger, slides it onto the stem of one red, blameless rose and leaves it there.

She takes her place, alone, and waits for consuming fires.

The Manchester Train

James Nash

He first saw the woman from the train. Her house was very close to one of the stations on his daily journey. One morning, as the train slowed down for the platform, he caught sight of her in her garden, patting earth in and around some plants she had planted in a large clay trough. It was very early in the day, and the April sky was a mother of pearl grey as if it promised rain. Some buds were bursting open like badly packed parcels on the black branches of a tree against the fence which separated the garden from the railway line. It was only a moment, but it seemed to him that their eyes met, and something was exchanged between them. He quickly put that down to his imagination, and an incorrigible romantic streak, unsuspected by any of his acquaintance, hidden deep beneath his impeccable dark suit. Though, often during that day in his Manchester office, when he should have been juggling the finances of his clients, he thought about her dark-eyed stare and the sadness he chose to see there. Overactive fantasy life, he told himself. She was probably just not properly awake yet. But he still thought about her.

It was weeks before he saw her again. But it gave him time to observe her house and garden, and to pick up more clues about her life. He learned to recognise the landmarks before the train reached Anna's little stone cottage, to look up from his laptop at just the right time. He called her Anna, it seemed to suit her somehow. He watched her garden gradually fill with green. During that month the daffodils gave way to a camellia which stood like a lanky show-girl by the kitchen door, with pom-poms of pink blossom all over it. A cold-frame later became filled with seedlings, which jostled together in their pots. Window boxes appeared on the downstairs window-sills, though not yet filled with summer plants. Sometimes there was washing on a line. So there was a child. A little girl, he guessed. But no sign of a man's clothes. Single? Divorced?

He began to examine himself a little more closely in his bathroom mirror, when he shaved every morning. His face, a stranger for many years, became more well-known to him. And a little hateful. He disliked the ordinariness of his features, the insignificant nose, the way that his eyes and mouth seemed to be slipping down his face. Once, he heard himself say above the sound of early morning Radio Four in his apartment, 'My name is Paul, and I'm forty-five. I have a great job, a couple of really good friends, and my life is terrific.' And his voice, loud and unconvincing, shocked him into silence again.

The truth was he was forty-five, and he felt exhausted. Exhausted by the blank walls of his new apartment (which he stubbornly called a flat) in the centre of Leeds, and exhausted by his daily journey to Manchester. Somehow she had pierced the bubble of his loneliness and made him feel, quite keenly, how alone he was. If he watched the television it seemed full of impossibly beautiful, and therefore unattainable, women. And when he went out into the city centre, there only seemed to be couples shopping, warm in shared intimacy, shutting him out. On one occasion, not long after he first saw Anna, he was buying himself some flowers in the market, when he saw a gay couple walking down one of the crowded aisles. They were chatting and laughing, and all the while seeking excuses to touch each other. He froze as one of the men turned and brushed a thread from his partner's jacket, and found he had crushed his bunch of flowers to himself, breathless with a sense of exclusion. When he got back to his flat, he found he had no vase for the gaudy carnations fringed with scarlet, and he put them in the sink. They stayed there for several days until he threw them away.

And then one morning she got on his train. At first he did not recognise her. She seemed larger, stronger, and less, what he, rather shamefacedly, thought of as feminine. He looked up from his work and several sheets of paper drifted to the floor. When he looked again she was already sitting. Her thighs were arched with muscle and strong in black trousers. Her hands were large and capable. She was wearing a dark red, embroidered velvet jacket, She stowed a big, black portfolio, the kind he thought vaguely that artists used, to the side of her, and started to read from a glossy magazine. She sat diagonally opposite him in the carriage, and he somehow recalled the spell she had originally cast over him all those weeks ago. It was still there, as powerful as the first time he saw her, once his memory had adjusted its image with the reality. She seemed to register his gaze on her and gave him the ghost of a polite smile, as if he almost wasn't there. It didn't bother him, because that was how he mostly thought of himself. Throughout the rest of his journey he carried on taking covert looks at her, and each time noticed more about her. She was older than he had first thought, and there were lines on her face. She had a big prow of a nose, so that her face in profile was like that of an empress on an ancient coin. Her hair was wound up away from her face and he saw her collar bone below the T-shirt neck.

He looked away and concentrated on his papers. Never had the rows of figures looked so boring. By the time they pulled into Manchester Piccadilly she was already on her feet, striding up the carriage to the door. He was aware of the power of her presence, and that other passengers were giving her covert looks. He stared over to where she had been sitting, stuffing his papers into his briefcase, and saw that she had left her magazine behind her. He reached over for it, and realised it was a catalogue for an art exhibition; at the same time he could feel the warmth of her body left on the seat, as elusive as a scent, and as erotically charged. On the back of the catalogue was a picture of her, perhaps taken several years before. She was an artist and it was her exhibition. Rhiannon Thomas. Not Anna then. He savoured her name on his tongue for a few seconds, and then he was off after her, off the train and up the platform, following her red jacket and the dark head bobbing above most of the others.

He caught up with her at the ticket barrier. She turned without seeing him, and he touched her shoulder.

'I think you left this behind.'

She looked at him with an initial cool politeness, the wattage and warmth of her expression growing as she realised what he was saying, and she took the catalogue from him. Her hands had no rings on them.

'Thanks,' she responded, 'that's very kind. I was supposed to be guarding it with my life. They're fantastically expensive to produce.'

And she smiled again, before turning through the barrier and walking out of the station. He stood for a minute almost reeling with the reality of the exchange. Her voice was deep and confident, and belying her Welsh name, she spoke in a kind of modified received pronunciation which he privately thought of as posh. Her gaze was direct and confident.

'Rhiannon Thomas,' he said aloud, and then repeated it.

He didn't see her for a few weeks. He spent the time in a kind of preparation for something. For something he did not name or identify, but something which spelled change in his life. He bought some new cutlery, with the intensity of someone who had never done so before, helped by a young woman who sold him two place settings for the price of a couple of nights in a luxury hotel. But he didn't allow himself to question what he was doing. Not even when he started wearing aftershave for the first time since he was nineteen, and chose a couple of new silk ties from Harvey Nichols. He became hopelessly aware of his collection of CDs, scattered across the wooden floor of his large living room, and started to put them back in their cases. And he looked her up on the internet.

She was relatively well known, he discovered, and the catalogue was for her sixth show, to be held in Manchester within the month. She was thirty-seven and had lived in San Francisco for five years. But nowhere was there mention of a partner or husband.

In the following weeks he got used to not seeing her. Occasional washing on the line reassured him that she was still living at the house. Her garden flowered and grew. One Saturday he went over to Manchester and saw her exhibition. He found himself confused by the shapes and colours she used, but was entirely swamped by the vivid quality of her artistic personality. It was as if she breathed throughout her work, and he remembered how the warmth of the train seat felt beneath his hand. He walked around puzzling over the images he saw on the walls of the little gallery. And then one stopped him in his tracks; it was the least abstract, seemingly a winter landscape of hills and wood, but having some of the quality of a reclining nude about it. It was all lush curves of brown and dark green, and its abandon made him light-headed. He drew closer to it, and felt her presence in the painting, her self containment and her sensuality. He had never bought a 'real' picture before and he dithered about whether he could afford this very small picture with a price tag of £1,750. When he went back during his lunchtime the following Monday, he found it had a red sticker on its frame indicating that he had not been quick enough. It had been sold.

Somehow it confirmed something about himself. And he said to himself, on his way back to his office, like a latter day White Rabbit, 'Too late, too late.'

And then one early evening, on his way back to Leeds, he saw her in the garden sitting at a picnic table, grass up around her ankles. A fleeting snapshot. She was smiling and talking to someone in the house. And in the doorway of the kitchen he saw her daughter for the first time. She was about eight, and she had a small puppy on a lead. The puppy was barking, and mother and daughter were laughing at each other across the garden, and then as if practising some unacknowledged ritual, both turned simultaneously and waved at the train.

He hugged their shared enjoyment to himself as he left Leeds station and walked up Wellington Street to his apartment. It had never looked emptier, in spite of the recent attempts he had made to make it more comfortable. He put on some music, the Goldberg Variations, and took off his tie. How was he to meet her again? He was pretty sure that he could find her house from the train station, but shied away from anything that might make him seem like a stalker. He would just wait. He would see her again.

He had one more tantalizing sighting of her walking the puppy around the garden on a lead, on his journey home, then suddenly quite unexpectedly she was on the train the next morning, sitting a few seats away. It was very crowded, and he had put his work away to give people more room. She looked in his direction and grinned at him, waving her hand a little.

And then her mobile rang. He heard her deep and well-spoken voice again, it was full of warmth and joy.

'Hi Tony,' she said, and he knew with a sinking of his heart that she was in love with the person she was talking to. There was a silence, and when she spoke again her voice was cracked, dry, and any youth had drained from it. All around her people shuffled, too close together, and trying not to listen. One elbow moving would disrupt the whole carriage.

'Oh Tony,' long sobbing intake of breath, 'oh Tony.'

And then she said, 'It's not your fault,' and then, 'it's not your fault. It's not your fault.'

He looked over at her, and her eyes were bright with unshed tears, as she continued.

'He was always trying to get out. I was in a constant worry about him getting on the road.'

She listened, spoke something reassuring in an undertone, and put her mobile back in her pocket. He was not surprised to see her get off the train at Huddersfield. Her dog was dead, and her partner was upset. Her daughter would need to be told.

It was a cold shower of reality. And so sudden he did not know immediately how he felt. But, he realized over the following weeks, it was a reversal he might have predicted. After that it was easier to spend all his journeys to and from work looking out of the other side of the train, away from her house, and away from her life. He hugged his loneliness to himself again like an old friend. He was not heartbroken.

Happy As I Am
Malcolm Aslett

I parked the van two streets away. Silly, really. I didn't want the other guests to see the painted sign on the side and brand me a *tradesman* straight off. Even left the blue tissue paper around the bottle of wine I was bringing because of some vague idea it looked more sophisticated.

It was evening and English summer cool. I was wearing my suit and felt the breeze quite noticeably on my legs through the thin material, so much so that when I got out of the van, just for an instant I thought I'd forgotten to put my trousers on.

The house was Victorian and gave a juvenile impersonation of a castle, with an affectedly complicated roofline and lancet windows.

There were small flat candles in jam jars laid on their side lighting a path to the back garden. The French windows were open wide and some tragic operatic duet was doing aural fisticuffs over the front lawn. As I approached, the volume dropped suddenly and I could hear voices inside.

Suze saw me hovering on the patio and came to greet me. She was barefooted, wearing a dress that was busily ethnic, suggesting more integrity than taste.

'Lenny, sooo glad you could make it,' she said while kissing me on both cheeks.

Her long black hair pushed against my face. The strands were dry and I could see the occasional grey threading the surface. I'm not being mean. I liked it. It added to her sense of worn elegance.

Besides, I make it a general rule to like the people who like me and she seemed to like me, even though we'd only met once before. Honest to God.

She'd seen my advertisement in the *Shields Gazette* and left a message with my wife who'd checked my calendar and pencilled her in. Just a small job. Her back door was jamming. I had a bit of trouble finding her as she'd only given the name of the house and the street. That's Boldon for you. It has nice bits where the solicitors and company directors live in quiet lanes hidden from the sight of the mucky commerce of Sunderland and Shields. Parts of it are posh enough to think they can do without a door number. I'm a terrible man for jumping to conclusions. I found myself building up a picture of a woman I hadn't even spoken to: a stuck-up middle aged mum with jowls like luggage handles, holding a poodle and wearing a year-round sunbed tan.

She wasn't stuck up at all. Nor the rest.

'It's this door here. I think it's the hinges,' she said, pointing to the rusted, broken hinge hanging by a single screw.

'I think you might be right,' I told her, and she looked pleased with herself and beamed as if this was going to be fun.

I fixed it in her kitchen because there was a hiccup of rain outside. It's a nice kitchen, a mix of old timbers and glossy metallic surfaces: *Upstairs Downstairs* meets *Star Trek*. But it looked lived in and comfortable with lots of crappy pictures by her three kids pinned up everywhere and jars of foreign foodstuffs cluttering the shelves. I propped the door on two saw horses and took the hinge off.

Sometimes people just leave you to these jobs. Others are afraid you might steal the family's chromium plated spoons and find a reason to potter around doing trivial tasks. Suze just wanted to talk.

She swept into a conversation that she may have been having with herself before I arrived, as if I could naturally take up her inner voice and answer her perplexities with the appropriate wisdom and compassion. I like that attitude that certain people seem to have; those who assume everyone is of the same clay. It flies in the face of reason to me, but it's a comfort to know such people exist.

She got on to the subject of an exhibition she was planning to see and interrupted herself to ask:

'Do you know Cezanne?' and sounded embarrassed.

'Of course,' I said. 'I watch television.'

She thought this was funny and laughed and did this cute thing with her head, rocking it to the left and right. It was such a girly thing to do it tickled me. Not to be misunderstood I started talking about Cezanne's childhood friendship with Zola and how odd and unlikely it was that two awkward boys who knew each other should each grow up to have such an international impact on their chosen crafts, as if the world really was a global village where we all knew each other's name and had an influence on each other's lives. You could see she was taken with the thought.

Talking about art for some women is the next best thing to erotica. It's like pressing a button labelled *Romance, Sacrifice, Mystery, Passion, Sex and Swiss Chocolates*. So when I finished the job and was tidying up, and she asked me if I'd like to come to dinner, I wasn't sure what she meant. I was on my knees with a brush and pan and paused to think it over.

'You can get to meet my husband, Eric. And there'll be all sorts of interesting people,' she clarified.

Don't get me wrong. I wasn't looking for an affair. I'm happy enough as I am. It's just exciting for me talking to a woman about things other than new clothes for the kids and where the money's coming from. Suze was – how can I put it without suggesting I was lusting after her? She was *appealing* to me. She had a clever, attractive face. You know the sort – no make-up, but spends the equivalent and more on soaps made from cocoa beans from the rainforests. Forty and proud of it. So I said yes and made an excuse for the wife not to be there. She would only have felt uncomfortable.

Suze's husband, Eric, tall with a tufty beard and shoulders that seemed to stop short of his arms came striding up behind her. He shook my hand with both of his, gripping it like he was squeezing water out of a wet towel and said, 'Wonderful to meet you, Lenny. Wonderful. That was such a marvellous job you did on the door. Marvellous. Wish I could do something like that. All thumbs I am. Look, sorry. I have to get the children to bed. Suze, darling, would you like to introduce Lenny to some of the others?'

Suze obliged and introduced me to a black woman who was studying their bookshelf as if it were the most fascinating bookshelf in the world and she a professional bookshelf appraiser from a family of professional bookshelf appraisers.

'Lenny, this is Grace. Grace is from Zambia.'

'I've never met anybody from that far away in the alphabet,' I told Grace. I shouldn't have said that but this woman was gorgeous. Tall and slender with extraordinarily large brilliant eyes and full lips. Her dress was a fluorescent lime colour. It hugged the lines of her body in a way that made you want to do the same. I immediately felt the need to impress her. I think if the tie I was wearing had been pure silk I would have shown her the label. Grace looked quizzically at me. She seemed worried I was insulting her. I looked about the room for inspiration to change the subject, at the two small clusters of guests gathered in haltingly polite conversations. Then I noticed the furniture had been pushed to one side, and a vast sheet of paper attached to one of the walls.

'Are you having the decorators in, Suze?'

Suze rested her hand on my forearm, rubbed it as if it were a magic lamp, and explained:

'I thought it would be nice to do something different for a dinner party. You know how awkward it all is, meeting new people and asking the same questions and having the same conversations.'

I nodded as if I was always going to dinner parties and then said, 'No.'

Suze laughed.

'Anyway. What I thought we could do was begin by painting a mural together.'

The room immediately felt colder, my underarms clammy.

'You can use anything you want: pencils, poster paints, acrylics,' Suze added quickly, as if she imagined any doubts I might have were to do with the availability of materials suitable to my creative urges.

'But what are we supposed to paint?' Grace asked, and she sounded pretty grouchy.

'No, anything. Anything!' Suze said, picking up a box of materials. 'That's the beauty of it. There is no *wrong* thing to paint.'

She offered me the box. I rooted out a 4H pencil and said the first thing that came into my head which happened to be, and I don't know why, 'You won't take *me* alive, copper.'

Grace looked so perplexed I felt sorry for her.

'Are we not eating now?' I heard a voice ask. It was a sulky looking lad in a baseball cap with a thin spotty face.

'We'll be having dinner after, Damian,' Suze told him sweetly.

'I'm hungry now,' he told her childishly.

'I have some snacks,' she said walking over to him. Then she rubbed his arm the way she had mine a few moments earlier. 'I'll fetch you some, shall I?'

There were ten of us in all, ill assorted as a bus queue.

'Right, we can start. *Anything*, you know. Anything you want,' Suze encouraged us before making a grand sweeping gesture with a four-inch brush to effortlessly paint an exquisite crimson arc a yard long on the virgin surface.

Suze's husband began by busily doing patterns around the edges. They were kind of nice. Bright blue whirly patterns. I started copying him when I saw how good they looked. Grace doodled away drawing small, ineffectual shapes in the corners and kept tugging at Eric's sleeve and asking him advice ('Does this look all right, Eric? How about *this*?'). A very small oriental woman who didn't seem to speak English and may have misunderstood everything started peeling the wallpaper off but stopped when Suze squawked and fell off her ladder. There was only one ladder and Suze had it most of the time. She needed it. Her big breasted mother figure lolling around a coconut tree took up most of a wall. An elderly couple with healthy outdoor faces had obviously been pre-warned. They were dressed in boiler suits and amiably crayoned in flowers and bunny rabbits under Suze's Mother Earth. Some guy in a wheelchair, plump and baby-faced but for a fine crop of blackheads that were sprinkled like pepper across his thin white skin, was propped uncomfortably to one side and painting dark shaggy figures with small withered legs which we all pretended not to notice. A woman called Bev who was a fairer, taller, wearier version of Suze opted for writing a poem in the manner of roughly drawn graffiti. I only remember a bit of the first line:

Eric read it at one point and responded ambiguously with, 'Extraordinary. I wish I could write.'

There was one more fella of course. Damian. I'm sure he was no more than eighteen and quite possibly a couple of years younger. He had several earrings going up the sides of each ear that reminded me of the shower rail in my sister's bathroom which she's never bought a curtain for. I don't mean to sound provincial but I think that's why this body piercing bothers me: it always looks like an unfinished job. It's so unprofessional. Damian was painting long brown sausage shapes before sloppily speckling them with white poster paint.

'Very artistic,' I said to him. 'Is it something Christmassy?'

'No,' he said without looking up, and chuckled. One of those Peter Lorre chuckles that bodes ill for all concerned.

Two long settees and three chairs were arranged in a U shape facing the wall, with two low tables through the middle to bear the food. We sat down to view our work while Suze and her husband went to fetch the food. Even Hieronymus Bosch wouldn't have dreamt this thing up. It was a lop-sided monstrosity, stretching from the *Garden of Eden* to the *Bronx* and shot through with Damian's long brown sausages that had ended up hitting Suze's big mother/goddess thingy like horizontal rain.

I was sitting between Grace and the old man who was gazing at the mural in admiration.

'Dreadfully good, don't you think?'

'The very word I was looking for,' I told him.

'Awfully good, what Suze has done,' said his wife. 'She's so full of ideas.'

Their overalls had been ironed with creases down the legs and both wore white cotton shirts with small neat collars. There was a quality about them: craftsmanship from a bygone age. The husband took out a pressed handkerchief and wet a corner to dab away a spot of Damian's brown poster paint from his old leather shoe.

'There's vegetable curry and ratatouille, pasta with tuna, pillau rice and nan bread, and a lamb korma for the carnivores,' Suze informed us as she and hubby arrived bearing trays the size of small pool tables. Eric filled our glasses. I didn't even see the bottle I'd brought. We were drinking organic red wine with little flecks of purple stuff that gathered at the bottom of the glass like tea leaves. If I'd opened it at home I'd have taken it back to the shop.

We weren't exactly conversing, more muttering with one another.

'Very piquant and such nice patterns on the plates,' I heard one of the oldies saying. Then Suze spoke up and asked Grace what she was doing at the university, and we all hushed up, like schoolkids caught talking by the teacher. Grace, choking down a mouthful of korma waved an arm in the air to gain time.

'I'm doing research into *Imperialist Strategies of Pedagogic Practices in Sub-Saharan Africa.*'

Bev, I noticed, simply nodded in that sad way parents do when they're talking about their teenage children. Been there, done that, nothing changes, all roads lead to misery, she seemed to say.

'Yes. But what is it about, exactly?' Suze persisted.

To be honest, I can't remember what Grace said then. I only know the title because she was asked to repeat it several times. I was wondering what we were all doing there. We were like the cast in one of those B standard disaster movies of the seventies. I was half expecting Karl Malden to walk in at any moment.

I checked out the paintings they had on their walls – no copies of Monet's *Poppy Field* here. All originals. A little gloomy, mind. Inky landscapes, crusty faces. Hardback books with bits of paper sticking out of them were piled haphazardly on surfaces. The music folios atop the piano had names on their spines you could namedrop: '*Fauré*', '*Delius*'. Potted plants with improbable looking leaves crouched in corners. The curtains had been left open. I could see stars appearing in the washed out sky behind the black trees. The wind was picking up and pushing around two tall cedars at the back of the garden. Eric filled all our glasses.

The conversation broke up into little pieces again. Craig, the one in the wheelchair, was in IT and hit it off with the oriental woman. She actually spoke English quite well in a one-to-one and was from Thailand or Taiwan or the like. Something with a T. They began discussing the joys of broadband.

Grace turned to me and asked me what I did. I told her I was a joiner.

'A joiner? What do you join?'

'I work with wood. A joiner. With hammers and nails and screws.'

She paused momentarily, before asking in a surprised voice, 'A carpenter?'

'Well, yes, if you like,' I said uncomfortably.

Then, without another word she turned her back to me and began listening to Bev who was in the midst of a long monologue explaining why she was glad ('*absolutely* ecstatic, really') that her husband had gone off with another woman ('Bloody good luck to them, I say.').

Damian was staring moodily into space when Suze decided he should have his moment.

'Damian?' she asked him sweetly across the length of the settee.

He jumped as if a dog had barked at him.

'Yeah? Wha…What?'

He had been holding his wine glass with one finger round the stem and as his hand twitched the glass tipped over and fell on the floor below a small table. He responded with a quick, 'Frigit.'

'Oh, I'm sorry,' Suze told him, 'My fault. I shouldn't have startled you.'

Damian's face flushed.

'S'a'right,' he responded ungallantly.

Suze soldiered on, 'I was wondering. Those curious shapes you painted. They're fascinating.'

'Oh aye?'

'You know, not that it matters, whether there is unity or not, but they do give the whole piece a kind of unity.'

'Oh aye?'

The old lady was nodding encouragingly. 'Yes. Yes,' she said, and seemed to mean it.

'Ehm, so. Are they meant to be anything in particular? Or are they abstract. Are they simply designs for their own sake?'

A drop of wine had landed on the armrest and he brushed at it lazily with his knuckles as he answered, 'They're meant to be something.'

Suze opened her eyes wide to encourage him.

'Yes?'

Her voice turned conspiratorial.

'When I was a lad and I'd come in from school, I'd ask me mam what we were having for tea. And every time I asked she'd say the same thing.'

'Which was?' Bev piped up, suddenly interested.

'Shit with sugar on,' he blurted. Then he laughed in a forced, squeaky voice.

At this point we all gazed back at the wall and realized what those long brown speckled streaks were meant to be.

'Oh,' said one of the oldies.

Suze's reaction was obscure. She smiled painfully and though it was a thin laugh it was a laugh nonetheless.

'How extraordinary,' she said.

Damian pushed himself up from the settee. His thin legs staggered a little and he had to put a hand on the armrest for support.

'What about your father?' Suze asked him out of the blue.

He stooped down and picked up the glass from under the table.

'Me dad? Him? I never speak to him. He says to me one time, "You're not *my* son."'

'You're not my *son*?' Suze quoted back in the form of a question.

'Aye. He said, "You're not my son, I'm not your dad."'

Damian paused a moment to pick up a wine bottle and poured himself a glass almost to the brim.

'He doesn't live with us no more. I stopped him in the street one time and he said that to me. I was so angry I wanted to hit him but I said, "I can't hit you because you're me dad," and he said "I'm not your dad." So I hit him.'

There were a couple of *Radio Four* gasps from around the table.

Damian shifted his stance clumsily and managed to step on Grace's toes and made her flinch. She looked over imploringly at Eric who then got up.

'Perhaps you might want to sit down, Damian?' he said and reached out a hand to grip the lad's elbow. Damian shrugged it off.

'You're not me dad either,' he told Eric sharply.

Eric reached forward again.

'I think you'd best sit down,' he repeated.

Damian's face contorted into a knotty smile before he struck him with the bottle. It was a girly, lazy swing and Eric had time to make a step backwards but it still caught him on the chin with a musical ping and just enough force so he toppled backwards into a small jungle of potted plants. Bev let out a shriek.

I got up straight away and grabbed Damian by the upper arm.

'Don't even think…' he started telling me. He waved his club in readiness so I thumped him in the stomach – not that hard, but a little low. He dropped to his knees and I loosened the bottle from his fingers.

Grace was helping Eric to his feet by this time. I looked over at Suze. She stood with her hands on her hips taking it all in. She didn't seem distressed. I can't say exactly what she looked. If it had been a drawing in a comic I think she would have had a little speech bubble coming out saying 'Hmmph!'

That pretty much wrapped up the dinner party though Suze and Eric surprised me again. They didn't sling Damian out on his ear but took him into an office room for an earnest discussion. Bev was left in charge of dessert.

Bev actually brightened up at this point. As soon as she had tables to clear away and a calamity to deal with she suddenly blossomed. She arranged taxis for those that needed them, provided coffee and cake while they waited, checked the kids were sleeping and tidied up the house. She was happy. She was like those racing cars with gears that only work well at high speeds, though in her case, it was her brain that seemed tuned for crisis.

The oldies left saying they had enjoyed the evening tremendously and to give the hosts their thanks. Almost out of the door, they remembered they had brought a camera and rushed back in to take a photo of the painting.

'Can't forget that, now can we?' the husband gleamed.

Grace hurried down the path to her taxi and looked as if she would go directly from the house into therapy. The man in the wheelchair, had his own van and gave the Oriental lady a lift, already acting like a couple.

Suze came into the kitchen while me and Bev were clearing plates away and informed us she was going to drive Damian home.

Bev asked, 'How's Eric?'

'Eric's going to have a couple of paracetamol and go to bed. He said to say sorry to everyone.'

'Why bother driving the lad home?' I asked.

'He lives in South Shields. He walked here, you know? It's miles.'

'I best come with you,' I told her.

'It's not necessary,' she replied evenly.

Bev intervened. 'It's probably best he does, Suze.'

The car was a four-wheel drive of some sort and Damian asked to sit in the front because he'd never been in one before. It was past 11pm when we dropped him off. He lived in one of the flats behind the shops at Horsley Hill. When we got out he gave Suze a big hug and she kissed him on the cheek and he started crying.

'I'm sorry, Suze. I'm really sorry,' he blubbered.

She patted his shoulder and made shushing noises. Then he turned to me and wiped his eyes and put his hand out to shake my hand.

'Sorry, mate,' he said. 'No hard feelings?'

His hand was still wet from the tears.

'Alright, son. Watch how you go,' I said to him.

'I only met him a couple of days ago,' Suze explained on the way back. 'He came round selling cleaning products. He said he was doing it to stay off the dole.'

'He came to the door selling Brillo pads and you invited him to dinner?'

It only occurred to me while I was saying it that I was pretty much in the same boat. I felt aggrieved. I thought I'd appeared special in her eyes and that she'd wanted her friends to meet me. Now I was on a par with a young thug who sold cream cleaners for a living.

'He seemed a nice boy. He was very eager. And I felt sorry for him. He can't be making much money.'

'Well, he's probably receiving social and earning extra with this job on the side.'

'No. No. He showed me his card. They get identification. A card with their photo on. It's some kind of Government project,' she told me heatedly. I bit my tongue. She deflated almost instantly. 'I feel it's all my fault,' she tiredly confessed.

'What's your fault? Him hitting your husband? How?'

'He's just young. And he drank too much. If I hadn't embarrassed him by asking those questions…'

'You can't blame yourself for him being a tormented teenager with a lousy home life.'

'No. I can. He was one of my choices.'

'What choices?'

'Oh. For the dinner. We get four choices – Eric and I – four each.'

'Guests, you mean?'

'Well, *yes*,' she told me, but it was an indefinite yes. She grimaced and went on. 'The dinners were my idea. It took me ages to get Eric to agree. And here he is getting *clunked* on the head with a wine bottle for his trouble.' Then she broke into giggles at the thought and put her hand over her mouth.

I told her, 'I can see you're cut up about it.'

She looked at me contritely.

'You must think I'm awful,' she said.

'No, I don't. Not completely.'

We stopped at a set of lights in Cleadon Village. Fine rain started to spatter the windscreen. She reached a hand over in the darkness and touched my thigh with her fingertips, a soft, affectionate prod.

'You know, we call them our pot-luck dinners.'

'Yeah?'

'We have them once a month. We have four choices each. We can invite anyone we meet – in a shop or in the street, or wherever. But they've got to be someone we don't know – they can't be, you know, established friends.'

'They've got to be strangers?'

'Mmm. Sort of.'

'What about Bev?'

'Bev.' She rolled her eyes. 'She's an exception. Since her partner left she gets a bit low without company. But other than that, no. Craig works at the university and had to fix Eric's computer recently. The Tippetts I met at an exhibition in Newcastle a couple of weeks ago. Kang's over on an exchange of some sort and met Eric at an open day last weekend. Then there was Damian. And…you.'

'What about Grace?'

'Oh, Grace? I forgot about her. Eric cheated a bit there. He's overseeing her doctorate.'

'That explains a lot.'

'It explains why she's shagging him.'

'Is she?' I asked, amazed.

She looked over and caught my eye. Then the lights changed and she put the car into gear and responded by pursing her lips.

'So what are these pot luck dinners in aid of?' I asked. 'Why not just have your own friends round?'

We pulled into her drive. She turned off the engine and she tucked one leg under the other so that she could turn sideways in her seat.

'It started last year after we got back from holiday in the Loire. We had Tony for dinner. I'd met him when we were visiting Anger. He'd asked me – in French – if I could take a photo of him but he was obviously English because he had a *terrible* accent and he was wearing a Sunderland football strip. But we got talking and it turned out he was a dustbin man – from Whitburn. Can you believe it? I know: they call them hygiene operatives nowadays or whatever it is but Tony simply says he's a dustbin man. And he was *absolutely* fascinating. He's been learning French at night school for four years and every summer he cycles in France so he can practise the language. He was *so* funny and *so* charming it made me think. I mean, there are all these amazing people and we don't ever get to know them because we only want people around us who are more or less paler versions of ourselves. Don't you think?'

Her question caught me off guard.

'I don't know. It's difficult to make new friends.'

'No, it isn't. No,' she insisted. 'No. You just have to be prepared to make friends.'

She looked at me eagerly, excited by the worthiness of her ideas. 'You'll have to meet Tony. You would really get on well with him. He's like you: interested in lots of things.'

I didn't know what to say and there was a lull.

'Would you like a coffee before you get going?' she asked and I felt the light touch of her finger tips again.

'Sure,' I told her.

Only the upstairs landing light was on. We crept into the kitchen and Suze started preparing coffees on a fancy looking espresso maker.

'I'm sorry if it was an awful evening for you,' she said.

'I enjoyed it.'

'Seriously?'

'Yeah. It was fun. Very different from my usual Thursday nights.'

She was smiling now.

'I wasn't sure if you enjoyed the art work.'

I laughed.

'Now that *was* a surprise. Is that what you always do? Have your guests do a *Muriel*?'

She came over, stood in front of me and brushed her hair back.

'That was actually the first time I'd tried that. Only, occasionally, it's been a bit awkward getting people to talk.'

'I can imagine.'

'Did you really enjoy it?'

'Yes. Mostly.'

She moved closer. She had put on a thick woollen cardigan for the car ride and I could feel it brushing against my shirt.

'So what did you like best?' she asked.

She was waiting for me to kiss her and so I did, pulling her towards me so she leaned against my body. She was so thin. Different from my wife who's a bit chunky these days. I can't remember the last time I kissed another woman. I suppose that's why it felt so special. Then a clunk on the stairs made us pull apart. Suze picked up two cups from the draining board as the door of the kitchen swung open.

'Lenny? Thought I heard talking,' Eric said as he shuffled in in his pyjamas. I could see the bruise on his jaw now. There was a bit of swelling that tipped his intelligent face onto the opposite scale and made him look dopey.

'Just having coffee. Do you care for some?' Suze asked him.

Eric opened the fridge and poured himself an orange juice, leaving the door slightly ajar.

'This'll do me,' he said, sitting down on a stool at the counter.

Suze went over and pushed the fridge door closed.

'How you doing?' I asked him.

'I've been better,' Eric said. 'I've been worse.'

It's really not a thing to be proud of, kissing another man's wife in his home. I wanted to get out of there. When the coffees were made I drank mine straight down.

'Best get going,' I told them.

Suze escorted me to the door. On the step she caught my arm and kissed me hurriedly on the lips.

'I'll be in the house on my own next Monday,' she said, and held my eyes.

'I'll see,' I told her.

I turned around at the gateway and saw her standing with her arms folded, watching me leave. I gave a wave but she didn't respond.

But no. I don't think I'll be round there on Monday.

Chunky wife and all, I'm happy as I am.

The Cocco-Bella Man

James K Walker

I am returning from a trip to Italy, compliments of a no-frills airline. Still slightly stunned that it has worked out cheaper than if I had got a couple of taxis in and out of my local town. I will spare you the shopping list descriptions of places 'you-just-must' visit as I have camcorder competent relatives, and I know it is boring. Besides, the world is something to be discovered, not something to be described and I have never been one for leaning towers or coliseums. They attract photographers and coach trips like Trafalgar Square attracts pigeons, and so you can't really see anything anyway.

What I am good for on my travels is attracting surrogate parenting. On this particular excursion an elderly couple took it upon themselves to watch out for me. Each morning they checked reception for my room key and seemed pleased when my missed breakfast was down to a hangover rather than a local headline declaring 'Tourist washed up by the sea'. Perhaps I have one of those faces that make others feel like I need looking after. Perhaps they were just lonely and missed their own children. They couldn't understand why I chose to travel alone just as I couldn't understand why they chose to be married for so long. Despite our differences we managed to occupy lifts and pass each other in hallways with the kind of civility one would expect from ancestors of the Victorians.

Most of my time was spent tanning. Like a typically greedy Brit I revelled in the consistency of the weather, but it was the solitude I enjoyed the most; being surrounded by hundreds of sunbathers who could not speak a word of English. There is a freedom in being deprived of oral communication. To bask in ignorance, to simply shake your head and shrug shoulders when asked a question allowed a temporary extraction from mundane social obligations. God, how I would love to roll over on to my belly every time my boss at work asked me a question or a stranger in the street asked for directions. All I knew was that every Italian word ended in a vowel and when you have a language as beautiful as this why on earth would you want to speak English?

During siesta the beach would empty and you wouldn't see another human for miles. I wondered what it would be like if nobody ever returned and the world remained this empty forever. I loved this time of the day most and just when the swarming Italians returned I would dive in the water until my eyes became so salty everything was a painful blur. The Italians were crazy fuckers and had no comprehension of danger. They dived and splashed and punched and kicked their way through the water. Later on there would be at least five moped accidents, as they drove exactly how they swam; impatient as if the world was about to end. The Italians who weren't swimming fondled each other under the water, and this preoccupation cut right across ages. It just wouldn't happen in England, well not as openly. In England it's all wind breakers and trying not to make a fuss. I cannot work out if the English are too reserved or the continentals too laid back. What I think I know is the environment you inhabit seems to shape the kind of person you become. Back in the cold wet of Britain with a hood up over my head and a scarf half covering my face I realise that I rarely see my skin. Is this why we deny our instincts so much, because we have forgotten what it is to be human?

On that beach, among the beautiful bodies that seemed celestially sculptured rather than bloodied and boned was a lonely figure. He was someone who didn't care to swim or have road accidents or sunbathe. He was the *cocco-bella* man. He would march daily up and down the beach covering miles upon miles of sand. If it wasn't for night falling I think he would continue shouting and walking until he entered a different continent where *beautiful coconut* no longer made vernacular sense. The *cocco-bella* man had crossed eyes which were perhaps the most crooked pair I had ever seen. Consequently, the poor bastard rarely sold a thing. Every time somebody shouted for his attention he would look up, be unable to place them, and so continue walking humming *cocco-bella* to himself.

He was far more interesting than ancient churches and monuments yet remained a surprising omission from *Lonely Planet* guides. He seemed pretty lonely to me with no-one to give his beautiful coconuts to. Back in Britain nobody is singing. Occasionally somebody shouts out 'Post' from behind a stand, but it's not the same. There is a distinct lack of vowels and besides, there is nothing beautiful in the prose of the local paper which prides itself on death, unemployment and crime.

Back in those Italian evenings I would sit alone in some piazza or other and think about the *cocco-bella* man. I would wonder if he was ever able to get *cocco-bella* out of his head. Did he sing it when in the shower, or did he count beautiful coconuts when he wanted to get to sleep? I could only begin to imagine what having to repeat the same words over and over again would do to a human. It would destroy you. I can see it now, out on a date.

'So what do you do for a living?'

'Cocco-bella.'

'What wine would you like?'

'Cocco-bella.'

'Do you want to come back to my place for a…'

'Cocco-bella.'

How did this guy cope in cinemas or restaurants when he had to sit still for a few hours in silence? And what if, God forbid, he had to attend a funeral? What if his occupation had created some kind of coconut related Tourette's?

'Ashes to ashes, dust to…'

'Cocco-bella.'

It must be an eternal struggle for him and I guess the *cocco-bella* man probably had more on his mind than the lifeguard on the beach whose only concern was waxing his legs and chest. How unfair our personal afflictions are.

As I sat in that bar an English couple came over and sat next to me, presuming because we shared the same dialect we could be friends. Unlike the old couple who were into universal parenting these two were into universal moaning and they wanted to sell me their life. They complained you just couldn't get chips and egg. That it just wasn't Spain; and that they liked sitting *inside* bars not outside all the time, although at least the cigarettes were cheap. As they talked at me, I looked ahead into the distance at the moon. It looked bigger than usual and was perfectly round. It was like a big hole and I wondered if I could swim up through the sky and out the other side when I eventually turned around, would the view be just the same?

After about twenty minutes of incessant yap, the couple realised that I had stopped listening.

'So where are you from?'

'Cocco-bella,' I replied.

'Pardon?'

'Cocco-bella.'

'I don't understand?'

'Cocco-bella.'

They started to laugh and looked a little nervous so I continued to repeat *cocco-bella* over and over again. Eventually they got up and left. It would appear, at the grand age of thirty-two, I had finally discovered something of use.

Now I am back in England and the familiar routine has set back in I often think of the *cocco-bella* man. I realise that he never had any intention of selling his coconuts he just wanted to walk up and down the beach in peace, singing to himself. Perhaps because he had crooked eyes it enabled him to see things differently, exposing the world for what it really is.

Now when my boss asks me to perform some humiliating mundane task, or a neighbour complains that I don't bring in my wheelie-bin, when the credit card companies try to get me to take out loans I don't need and strangers decide to vent spleen as we queue up to pay for shopping, I think of the *cocco-bella* man. I try to see the world from his perspective and I translate their words into a mellifluous tone. *Cocco-bella, cocco-bella, cocco-bella,* and the world suddenly becomes a more bearable place.

Wonderwall Authors

Penny Aldred lives in West Yorkshire. In 2004 she won first prize in the Northern Echo/Orange short story competition and also in the Boston Standard flash fiction competition. Publications include stories in *Eclectica* (online) and in *Aesthetica*. She is a member of Alex Keegan's online writing group.

Malcolm Aslett was born in South Shields and educated in the north. Malcolm now lives in Buckinghamshire. He is married with a son. His story 'Crumpet' was included in *Naked City*.

James Bones was born and grew up in Warrington, studied cybernetics at the University of Bradford and is currently working towards an MA in writing at Liverpool John Moores University. He has worked in call centres, warehouses, IT and a comic book shop.

Sarah Butler was born in Manchester and currently lives in London. Despite her love of mountains she seems drawn to the flat lands of East Anglia: she read English Literature at Cambridge University and took an MA in Creative Writing at UEA in Norwich. She has worked as a literature development officer in Leicester and spent time living and working in Canada, Romania and South Africa. She now combines a part-time post working for a literature project in East London with her own writing.

Crista Ermiya is of Filipino and Cypriot-Turkish parentage, and grew up in Hackney, London. She moved to Newcastle-upon-Tyne in 2002. She is a co-editor of *Other Poetry* magazine and recently set up indie poetry press *dogeater*. This is the first publication of one of her short stories. Like everyone else she has met in Newcastle, Crista is currently working on a novel.

Alexandra Fox lives in a village near Northampton. She caught the short-story bug in 2004 and now has more than a dozen first prizes and many placings and publications, including a Notable Story 2004 nomination in Absinthe Literary Review, and a story in Virgin Atlantic's in-flight magazine. Alexandra writes with Alex Keegan's online Boot Camp.

Philip Hancock was born in Newchapel, Stoke-on-Trent in 1966 but now lives in London. His poems have appeared in magazines including: *Orbis*; *The Rialto*; *Tears in the Fence*; *The North*; *Other Poetry*; *Smoke*; *South* and *Smiths Knoll*. Previous short stories appeared in Route's *Next Stop Hope* and a byteback book: *Old School Ties*. He is currently working towards his first collection of poems and developing an idea for a radio play.

Tania Hershman is a science journalist, originally from London and now living in Jerusalem with her partner and two cats. Science and short fiction are Tania's twin passions. *The White Road*, which was broadcast on BBC Radio Four in 2005, is part of a collection of short stories each inspired by articles from *NewScientist* magazine. To pay the rent, she writes articles about Israeli science and technology, all the while longing for that enormous advance that short story writers get so often these days so that she could give it all up and just write fiction. Tania's published articles and fiction can be found on her website, www.taniahershman.com

Carolyn Lewis has been published by *Mslexia*, *QWF*, the *New Welsh Review*, *Honno*, *Accent Press* and *Libbon* magazine. In 2001 she won the Lichfield Prize, in 2002 she won the Phillip Good Memorial Prize and in 2005 she came second in the Mathew Prichard Award. In 2004 she graduated with an MPhil in Writing from the University of Glamorgan. Carolyn lectures part-time in creative writing and conducts workshops in local secondary schools. Although born in Cardiff, she now lives in Bristol.

Jennifer Moore is a 29 year old Cambridge English graduate now settled in Devon. She combines writing with looking after her two young children. Other publications include a short story in *The Guardian* and some non-fiction articles on witchcraft.

Michael Nath has published short stories in *STAND*, *Critical Quarterly*, *Billy Liar* and *Main Street Journal*. Michael has written two novels, *British Story* and *The Book of the Law*, and is at work on a third, *La Rochelle*. He has lectured at five universities.

James Nash is Writer in Residence for Leeds University, Faculty of Education, and for High Schools in Calderdale. He is a freelance writer and edits a poetry column in *The Leeds Guide*. His third collection of poems *Coma Songs* was published in 2003 to great acclaim. With an increasing portfolio of published short stories, he is at present working on his first novel.

James K Walker lives in Nottingham and is currently researching a book entitled *If Brian Clough had been my Father* which is due for publication in 2006. Information on this and other work can be found at www.jameskwalker.co.uk

The Route Series

*Route publishes a regular series of titles
for which it offers an annual subscription.*

Wonderwall (Route 16) is a title in the Route Series.
For details of the current subscription scheme
and our complete book list please visit:

www.route-online.com

Naked City

(Route 15)

ISBN 1 901927 23 7

£8.95

'The eclectic, the humorous, the heartbreaking, the psychological, the fear and angst are all here in a collection that not only embodies the city but occupies the very soul of the urban landscape.' - **Inc Writers**

'This collection suggests that the short story is making a spirited comeback.' - **Nottingham Evening Post**

'Punchy, pithy and darkly humorous.' - **Liverpool Daily Post**

'If you want to keep abreast of current reflections on social and sexual change and expose yourself to some top-quality storytelling, this is the book for you.' – **Juice Magazine**

'Naked City is indeed an intriguing insight into city life and the people living in it.' - **Manchester Evening News**

At the heart of the modern city we find stories of lovers, stories of people with a desire to connect to someone else, something else. This collection reveals the experience of living through changing times, of people shaking the past and dreaming of better days, people finding their place, adapting to new surroundings, laughing and forgetting, living and loving in the grip of the city.

Included are a series of naked city portraits as seen through the lens of photographer Kevin Reynolds and a selection of the very best in new short fiction in a bonus section, *This Could Be Anywhere*.

Jack and Sal

Anthony Cropper

ISBN 1-901927 21 0 £8.95

Jack and Sal, two people drifting in and out of love. Jack searches for clues, for a pattern, for an explanation to life's events. Perhaps the answer is in evolution, in dopamine, in chaos theory, or maybe it can be found in the minutiae of domesticity where the majority of life's dramas unfold. Here, Anthony Cropper has produced a delicately detailed account of a troubled relationship, with a series of micro-stories and incidents that recount the intimate lies, loves and lives of Jack and Sal and their close friend Paula.

Next Stop Hope - Route 14

ISBN 1-901927 19 9 £6.95

A title in the route series, presented in three distinct collections: *Criminally Minded*, *Something Has Gone Wrong in the World* and *Next Stop Hope*. Featuring new short fiction and poetry from thirty-three writers.

Warehouse

MS Green, Alan Green, Clayton Devanny, Simon Nodder, Jono Bell - Ed Ian Daley

ISBN 1-901927 10 5 £6.95

Warehouse is a unique type of social realism, written by young warehouse operatives from the bottom end of the labour market in the middle of the post-industrial heartland, it steps to the beat of modern day working-class life. A soundtrack to the stories is included on a complimentary CD, warehouse blues supplied by *The Chapter* and urban funk grooves from *Budists*.

One Northern Soul

J R Endeacott
ISBN 1-901927 17 2 £5.95

If that goal in Paris had been allowed then everything that followed could have been different. For young Stephen Bottomley something died that night. *One Northern Soul* follows the fortunes of this Leeds United fan as he comes of age in the dark days of the early eighties.

The Unexpected Pond

Editor - Chris Firth
ISBN 1-901927 05 9 £5

Twenty stories to unsettle the complacent mind. This is a collection that is both challenging and healing. The Unexpected Pond is a book to unlock the imagination with a collection of stories focused on the bizarre, outlandish and macabre. These stories with their unexpected twists, turns and unusual premise, take the reader to the extremities of the mind and back again, through darkness into light.

Tubthumping

Editor - Adrian Wilson
ISBN 1-901927 17 2 £6.95

Pioneering short story collection that was the initial force behind the Route imprint. Human preoccupations - love and hate, anger and betrayal, lust and longing - are played out against a panoramic backdrop that would have been inconceivable before now. With an introduction by Alice Nutter.

Apocalypse Not Just Now

M Y Alam

The collected articles of M Y Alam 2000-2001. In this period he suffered a short period of unemployment, watched TV in bed, listened to music and grew disillusioned with being a writer. He pointed the finger at whatever and whoever he didn't like the look of. When events on his own doorstep and around the world turned sour, there was an added gravitas to his writing but his line of argument remained remarkably consistent. A compelling snapshot of a time which saw euphoric millennial optimism give way to a much more pessimistic introduction to our new, golden millennium.

Four Fathers

Editor: Tom Palmer

A tender and heartwarming collection drawn together from four sons who have reflected on their fathers, themselves and what fits between. Includes writing from Ray French, John Siddique, Tom Palmer and James Nash. With an introduction by Jim Sells of the National Literacy Trust.

Love of the Wild and Wayward

Mandy MacFarlane

Mandy MacFarlane has produced a distinctive collection of fables and modern folk tales that get straight to the heart of relationship complexities and breezes through them with a power and clarity that comes only with this, the most original form of story telling. It is true, there is a much more life affirming alternative to the current plague of chic lit, and this is it. Put away the chardonnay and pick up a full-bodied red.

The Trouble With Love

Various

Better to have loved and lost than never have loved at all – so it goes. But when love departs it can leave a hollowness that was not there before it came. The four stories collected here know the trouble that love can bring. Featuring stories from Susan Everett, Steve Dearden, Julie Mellor and Yolande Knight.

East of No East

Editor: Daithidh MacEochaidh

Four short stories from leading Bulgarian writers; Zdravka Evtimova, Boyan Biolchev, Svetlana Dicheva and Dimitar Tomov. A young woman looks after an elderly lady who has promised to bequeath her beautiful apartment to a person willing to take care of her until death; in a cemetery a funeral is delayed while gravediggers finish their digging; a young homeless boy dreams of cherry orchards as he works a cheese-patty stall to pay the rent in order to sleep in a corner of an underpass; and a dancing bear breaks free from its retirement in search of its owner and to dance again.

Bitter Sky

Zdravka Evtimova

A sequence of short stories following the fortunes of Mona, the precious only daughter of Rayo the Blood, this is a warm and highly rewarding piece of storytelling from one of Bulgaria's leading writers. Bitter Sky reveals the nature of power and vanity in all its complexity and plays witness to the transformation of Bulgaria from a former part of the Eastern Block to part of the emerging new Europe.

Old School Ties
Philip Hancock

In these stories, painter, decorator and poet, Philip Hancock looks with an emotional eye at the sadness at the heart of small town England, where old school friends never leave but remain scattered like debris; an ever present reminder of lost promises and faded ambition. This is a book for the lost child within us all and our quests to reclaim a very particular kind of love.

The Three and a Half Day Parent
James K Walker

A young father is happy to be a split-parent, half a week he looks after his son, the other half of the week he 'does drink'; a situation he advocates as a pragmatic way forward for the future of parenting. In this mini-collection of stories, a series of adult encounters with children in various scenarios have the cumulative affect of strengthening this case. *The Three and a Half Day Parent* is a funny and affectionate look at the relationship between adults and their children and will have you chuckling with recognition from start to finish.

*Byteback books are a new book format which is designed to be downloaded from the Internet, think hardback, paperback and now, byteback. Byteback books are actual books, printed on paper.

Full details of our book programme
and order details can be found at:

www.route-online.com